Welcome To

New Edge Hill

By Dani Brown

Morbidbooks.Wordpress.Com

Morbidbooks/facebook.com

Dani Brown

Welcome To New Edge Hill

ALL STATIES SHOULD DRIVE CADILLACS. It was suggested by myself. Then a detective even more uncool than me suggested a Volvo. The Force had no say over our personal vehicles but 'cop cars should match' was the argument we were both shot down with. We were then told about the merits of shaving by our superiors. My straggly beard tried to become ingrown at the thought of a razor.

I found myself being driven around by this same uncooler-than-me detective the very next week. His real name was Theodore Richards, but he'd been christened Teddy Dick five minutes after joining the academy.

There were strange goings-on out in the mountains, with strange lights spotted in the sky (obviously my superiors had not heard of drones). No other cop would touch it, and we were reliably informed that there were Prohibition Era barber shops and beard cream stores in the towns on the way. We could stop at each and every one if we so desired.

We argued about what to listen to the entire way to our destination, which was unclear to begin with – we assumed it would be when the potholes merged into endless holes, gravel roads with fences of mutant trees and dilapidated houses being chocked by the undergrowth. My taste in music was much more obscure than his. Even if his beard was longer and his moustache had sharper points, I was the true unique person. The other cops felt threatened by our willingness to be ourselves and live by our rules. We would be stuck with all the pointless investigations with the same arguments about what to listen to on our way.

I doubt even ten others had heard of my favourite bands, which were probably only ever heard of by other bands, musicians and their girlfriends, boyfriends, significant others, sycophants until I unearthed the hidden cache of cassettes at the dump while digging for a typewriter and Polaroid film (neither of which could be found with my metal detector for some reason – the typewriter should have sent it into overdrive). Teddy refused to hear my argument. Even other cops had heard of the trash he wanted to play. He won because he was driving. He was driving because he was the detective and I was the cop.

The further towards the edge of civilisation we drove, the stranger things became. Maybe my superiors had heard of drones after all. This might even be an actual investigation rather than the case of the missing doughnuts we were sent on last week.

My attempts to engage him in conversation were met with silence and beard twitching. It was vital knowledge I wanted to share with him. He saw it as ideal chit-chat – fantasising about different ways to fashion his 'tash was more important. I wish I tried harder to share my knowledge with him and check to make sure he was engaging with what I said. It was more like I was talking at a brick though.

Electricity danced on the air but there was no storm. My body hair swayed with it. Insects that only lived in my imagination crawled all over me urging me to scratch. Teddy would have some sort of snide comment if I acted on it. I sat on my hands instead.

Without a word Teddy Dick switched off the music and put on the weather advisory service. Relief washed through me; he could sense it too, whatever it was. I hope invisible insects were walking across his body too. There was nothing apart from blue skies and low humidity for hundreds of miles.

My vast knowledge culled from hidden conspiracy theory forums cried out all at once. Each fragment of information wanted to be heard. Shouting in unison, I could not focus on any particular thought.

Lightning bugs that usually rested in the day now flickered in the gloom under the bright sky trying to attract a mate. They were the only real bug around. Not even an angry yellow jacket had flown into the car in search of the most painful place to plant its sting, as usually happened when Teddy Dick was driving (he did not like air conditioning).

The information gleamed from the hidden net had something to say in the matter. I needed to slow it down before I could process (I was beginning to think like Teddy Dick – too much time in each other's company). There was something in my vast array of knowledge in there about insects disappearing. I also required a call-back to insects changing habits.

The road was paved – I had driven on it hundreds of times before yet it took on more dust than an old Western film. Teddy had to use the windshield wipers to wash it away. I had never seen Death Valley but that was what went through my mind upon seeing the dirt washed up.

The weeds dotting the side of the road had a dusty quality about them too. Dying, some already decayed and ready to enter the earth as nutrients for the dry soil, I did not trust them – they looked somewhat carnivorous, yet without the taste for flies. They were the most unnerving thing of all. It was like they had eyes.

I believed it to be some type of ruse designed to lure us into a false sense of security; belief that there was nothing to see here, move along, move along. The weeds watched us as we drove past. Their vines stretched towards the tires, upset they could not reach us without being run over. Two granola eating Staties wouldn't have tasted nice anyways but they didn't know that.

Welcome To New Edge Hill

I would trade Teddy for someone hiding behind a screen name any day. They would want to investigate, take pictures and upload them right away. Everyone on the forum would have something to offer to the investigation. For Teddy, unless it was white gel for his beard, it did not exist.

A bird called overhead shattering the silence. I did not notice when Teddy Dick switched off the weather advisory service. When he drove, I tuned out what blared out of the speakers. Only when he switched the radio off did it add to my overall unease. Certainly not a situation the rest of the force would purposely put us in – the teasing was only ever in jest and good nature – everyone needed someone to pick on. That did not make it any less tiring.

Not even the hillbillies sat on their porches watching us with glassy eyes. They were, like the radio, noticed only by their absence. They were usually disturbing – lack of them I now considered to be worse.

The lack of locals would set the entire forum on edge. Empathy was found in vast quantities in the close-knit circle of conspiracy theory forums on the dark web. It was something I did not get in the real world. Although this world me and Teddy found ourselves driving through did not seem real – it seemed like a copy, a poor one at that with far too many things missing for my comfort.

Me and Detective Teddy were the butt of the Force's jokes. All their jokes. Each and every day. But this job seemed like the most pointless thing they could come up with this morning when it was handed to us and so far, we had not seen a barber shop – Prohibition Era or otherwise. There would be some sort of "gotcha" waiting for us in the boons, complete with toilet paper used as party streamers (thankfully none of them were gross enough to consider using used toilet paper). The hillbillies were in on the joke too. A test to see if we could solve an actual case.

It seemed the most logical explanation. The one I yearned for. But I knew it was not so. I clung onto the belief for as long as I could. Around the edges, conspiracy theories and odd past occurrences creeped into my thoughts.

Our old partners had disappeared. There were a lot of disappearances in these parts – a bid for freedom somewhere less isolated. That's how I found myself teamed with a detective. The only other hipster on the force, or the only other person out of the hipster closet. But we never referred to ourselves as hipsters except in our own heads. Since that time, we had been sent on more wild goose chases in the boondocks than I care to remember.

Welcome To New Edge Hill

It was hard not to think of my old partner. The disappearance of him was what drew me into the murky world of online conspiracy theorists and cryptozoologists to begin with. There were many disappearances before then and many since but it was that one that had the impact. I worked with him every shift so it could not be down to a teenage runaway (he was nearing retirement and looking forward to it). A part of my mind chalked all the other disappearances to teenage runaways, junkies and people looking to escape.

We still did not like each other all that much deep down but outwardly we pretended. In a great show of pretentiousness and assholery we feigned friendship so our peers could have their jokes. I was even given an invite to his daughter's birthday party which I accepted (and provided her with a bucket of garish ponies).

The dislike was something that could not be explained away by simple hipster rivalry. After all, we could not admit to being hipsters (but we were free to refer to the other as being a hipster). I suppose we both missed our old partners.

My moustache twitched in an effort to escape the confines of a bucket of cream, hair ointment and the extensions I had put in last week. It wanted to compete with Teddy's natural face locks and show that it, too, could stand proud.

Dani Brown

The hair on my arms had only run of the mill body lotion to keep it in place, which in the unexplained circumstances I found myself in with Teddy Dick that late summer morning, was of complete uselessness. It stood up on end.

I looked over at Teddy. The desire to see a facial hair out of place, snap a picture and post it online was too strong to resist. But his face hair was perfect, as always, leaving my heart to sink and ponder what I must look like (I refused to confirm my suspicions by looking in the mirror). The hair on his arm closest to me was in a state similar to my own. At least not everything about him was perfect. It was confusing that someone could be so perfect and yet, still be such a dickhead.

I kept expecting the missing locals to jump out of the bushes and from behind the trees and yell "surprise", armed with tweezers and hot leg wax – another prank at our expense. The thought did not explain the discomfort though. Somewhere deep down inside I knew the locals would not be doing that.

Myself and Teddy should form an alliance and swap Gameboy games. But jealousy was my mistress. Those moustache points were worth every bit of my envy. He could stab someone with them – a knife on his person without a chance of arrest or a fine. I knew the answer for what was going on here lurked on the conspiracy websites I was so fond of.

Welcome To New Edge Hill

Mindless chit-chatter about Gameboy games would offer distraction from what was going on outside the car. Becoming friends with Teddy would mean less time for the Internet. It would mean I would get some sleep. I hadn't had a full night's sleep in weeks.

The deeper into the middle of nowhere we drove the more unnerved I felt. His arm hair implied Teddy felt it too but it was a topic not open for discussion. Nothing was open for discussion with Teddy ever. He was such a depressing person to be around. He was thoroughly boring too. Life with him on the force was all beard cream and Prohibition Era barber shops.

We weren't given instruction on what we were looking for except the barber shops and beard cream stores ("wall-to-wall, floor-to-ceiling creams for face pubes" was how one aging cop, a doughnut away from a heart attack, put it). Our superiors said the lights had been spotted near one but there were reports of the drone-like lights from all over the boons. Hillbillies obviously liked their drones – there was much else to do out here past the edge of civilisation.

The weather advisory service chimed into life for one brief second with both of Teddy's hands on the steering wheel and mine beneath my bottom. Without any static, it switched off. There was no boom to signify the radio blowing out. Just off. I pressed the button to turn it on – another exercise in the pointless. Truth be told, I did not believe Teddy Dick had noticed. If it weren't for the seat belt restraining me I would have jumped into the air and banged my head on the roof. I had something of a delayed reaction and ended up with a graze to cut into my freshly laundered and pressed uniform shirt.

The car sounded like it was not running; we continued our forward trajectory in silence. Complete and absolute silence pressed down upon me, yet it could not push my hairs back down. If I was not so creeped out I would have found that to be rather annoying. My friends behind the screennames would have found one million different explanations; at least half of them would have related to aliens with the remainder related to the government or shadowy secret government that controlled the puppets voted for by the public and paraded in front of the cameras.

The bird's call was never answered. It could have been snatched out of the sky by one of the mysterious lights we were sent to investigate. The longing for loneliness was enough to make my eyes water. No sounds suggested nothing was around but I sensed otherwise.

Being a passenger, I could not remove my foot from the gas pedal and discover if we could coast up the hill. There was little chance of Teddy experimenting –

for a detective, he lacked the curiosity that would have landed him the job. A rumble rocked the car. It wasn't thunder. The sound made me think the weeds were giving birth. Another sign of wishing myself and Teddy were in actual fact entirely alone.

Teddy Dick informed me of his ravenous state and intention to pull over for Salisbury steak and mashed potato. The rumble of his stomach was loud enough to echo in the silence. His choice in meal seemed more school cafeteria and less detox smoothie and granola. I'm sure if he trusted me, he would have insisted it be washed down with micro-brewed hard cider. For all I knew, he was the one not to be trusted. The people behind the screennames suggested he might have an alien parasite controlling him and sucking out his brain through his beard.

His words echoed out of the unrolled windows and off the dusty houses. No one came out to offer Salisbury steak or even to see what the two cops were up to. Even the sight of a local would have been welcome. They could have explained the pressing feeling of being watched despite there being no one else around – not even an animal. I may have recognised someone from the forums with a secret agreed signals. Conspiracy theorists liked living in the middle of nowhere. It was safer.

Dani Brown

Inbred children with webbed feet should have run between the houses looking for a gaming device that works. Upon seeing the cop car, they should have chased us with forest chickens following behind them. But there weren't any children (or any chickens or forest fowl of any variety).

The only things to be heard apart from his desire for Salisbury steak were the weeds. Their roots stretched deep. They did not seem natural; such a far cry from what choked my flower beds despite being of the same species, same size, same everything – they could not be natural. If we have been sent out all this way to examine creepy weeds and bring back samples I'm going to be mighty mad. They seemed the type to spew random lights high into the air and cause panic amongst the locals.

Teddy Dick hummed under his breath without any respect for the pressing silence and creeping weeds. The still air echoed his intention to stop for Salisbury steak and mashed potatoes, informing anything within a ten mile radius of our location. But that was not enough noise for Teddy. The weeds did not need the alert – they had eyes.

In a desperate plea to make him stop I slapped his arm. The resultant echo was loud enough to give our location to anyone (anything) who desired it within a twenty mile radius. I did not think there was any person or animal around...but there was something. I shrank back into my seat. Dozens of conspiracy theories danced across my mind chased by creatures in the deepest cryptozoology forum.

I wanted to be out of there but knew his stubbornness would mean we would not stop until we found a barber shop and beard cream store – Teddy's way of having the last laugh. There would not be one. On a normal day he would be able to have his Salisbury steak and mashed potatoes drowning in gravy at any roadside diner.

This far into the boons I doubted there would not be any Prohibition era barber shops or beard cream stores but Teddy did not want to acknowledge that, even though he knew it too (unless his beard was eating his brain at a more rapid pace than I initially thought). I wonder how many cocks he'd had to choke on to make detective; he obviously did not get the job through smarts or intuition.

Nomadic, he did not have any family on the force (or even in the state) to give him a leg up either. He was Teddy Dick before the beard came in. His wife was not much smarter. She was hot. He was hot. They must have some really pointless conversations when they're both alone. She did not have any close family either, as far as I knew.

Dani Brown

My friends in the forums could think of every possible explanation for any situation but they could not think of Teddy Dick's deal. He made no sense. The force made no sense in hiring him. Nothing made any sense.

A hipster should not be allowed to be a detective – loose whiskers had the potential to contaminate crime scenes. It made no sense. So many other candidates, better qualified with more intelligence must have been passed over for him to get the job.

I knew to keep my mouth shut. Teddy Dick was not one to be argued with. He could shoot down anyone with a few choice words regardless of the pointlessness of his argument and the flaws it contained. I suppose that was an intelligence of sorts. A more intelligent person would accept what he already knew; there was not going to be a Prohibition Era barbershop or beard cream store.

The sky pressed down on the roof of the car despite the miles of clear blue overhead. There was a distinct possibility of being crushed to death. An ice scrapper would be required to get my body off the road – once I was released from the car. Unless the weeds liked pressed juice. Then there would be no bodies to scrape. I wanted to snap a picture and upload it with the forum's hashtag of the day but I lacked the signal.

The weeds followed the car with whatever served as their eyes. It was the only explanation for the feeling of being watched unless the empty houses grew eyes out of their wall tumours. The hairs standing up on my arms told me the houses did not have teeth.

I was well on my way to madness in the passenger seat. The worst part was feeling the sky pressing down on me. Teddy Dick did not notice the world outside the windshield closing in. My theory involved his beard sucking the brain cells from his head. How else could it be so soft and shiny, silky smooth? I lacked the words to describe it in the forums. If I had them, the people behind the screennames would not need any other explanation for him and therefore the seeds of doubt with have never been transplanted into my mind.

The scenery outside changed; the wooden houses grew further apart with more trees between them and the occasional remains of something built out of stone (a wall, maybe or even part of a house).The porches were further back from the road, still visible and still sagging beneath one hundred years of feet and weather. They were vacant.

A lonely ball bounced on a driveway – a sign that people should be here. A weed sent a vine towards it but it could not play basketball. Not everybody would have run into their house at the same time. During the dog days, children should be seen playing outside, or at least watching Netflix on their porches. They'd be dressed in dusty rags this far out in the boons.

The ball bounced without anyone there to bounce it. Teddy Dick pulled up to watch it. If he saw a glimmer of someone there he did not say anything to me about it. Even if there was a glimmer, the cause would have been related to his excessive use of beard cream.

My bowels turned to liquid when he called out. Clenching, a silent prayer was said to whatever god or gods, demons, angels, whoever might have been listening, to return it to its solid state before I experienced leakage. Someone seemed to be listening because the sensation soon passed.

Teddy Dick did not give his voice a chance to echo before calling out again. The desire to knock him out and cuff him with his own cuffs was almost too strong to swallow down. Swallowing might have a laxative effect – something best avoided at that very point in time – but I had to.

I took out my Gameboy instead – the volume turned down, with the hope that my bowels would stay inside. I could not risk a disciplinary. The grey images dancing across the screen transported me to a different world. The passing of time changes while gaming, even on an old handheld that requires a rucksack of spare batteries and external light source. Risking coolness with a 3D handheld was worse in my mind than a disciplinary; anything newer and rechargeable and I ran the risk of being considered mainstream. Not only would I lose creditably with the folks in the retro stores, I would lose it online too.

I don't know how long I was hunched over before the batteries started to give way. We were moving again. The desire to knock Ted out had passed – there was no point in replacing them. The need to take in my surroundings was more important than changing batteries.

The houses were further back from the road and few and far between. The car climbed. There was not a Prohibition era barber shop or beard cream store. I had come to the conclusion that Teddy Dick would drive right over the mountains and down the other side until he arrived at one.

The sign, tucked behind some overgrowth but with enough letters visible to make out the words, read WELCOME TO NEW EDGE HILL. I had never heard of it before but there were a lot of places I had never heard of – map reading was not something I considered to be a hobby. New Edge Hill could be assumed to be one of those inbred villages at the foot of the rounded mountains populated by web-footed brother-cousins and sister/half-brother husband/wife teams (also with webbed feet). I added wondering what happened to Edge

Hill to the stuff chasing conspiracy theories around in the back of my mind.

The inbred were not anywhere to be seen. They should have been watching us with their beady eyes poking out from under long hair and dirty faces. If they were watching from behind their dirty windows I would have felt them in the same way I could feel the weeds pressing into my uniform and undressing me, before they discarded their fantasies upon discovering we did not share cousin genes.

The car hiccupped and stalled. Automatics should not do that and when they do, it should always be on the railroad tracks. Teddy Dick could not get it started. I told him to get out and let me try, using more hand signals than words. What words I did use bounced around until they became something else. He was reluctant to give up the wheel. Like a spoilt brat he tried to get the words out but found himself too exasperated. I would hate to be his significant other. He must be a chore for his wife to please in bed; he probably moans with bitchiness rather than pleasure.

Just when I was about to give up, he stepped out of the car. The impression I received was it was his intention to walk up the pathetic rounded mountain in search of Prohibition era barber shops and beard cream stores. If I could get the car started I would leave him there to continue his quest alone with the weeds. And when he arrived at the station a week later because he'd kept going in search of the barber shop, he would insist I be fired. My ability to care simply was no longer there. We were meant to be a team but it was hard when we despised each other to the point of not listening. If he was capable of strong emotion – I think the beard cream may have sucked that out of him.

The desire to be out of the creepiness, wearing my long underwear while sat in front of the air conditioning unit was strong. I could always start up on my own as a self-employed shoe shine boy. Hell, being a butt-lick boy ("Suck shit outta your ass! Five dolla!") would be preferential to being stuck in some inbred village beyond the boons. I had to bring in enough income to keep me in my retro items of obscurity.

Teddy Dick did not seem to mind – as long as he did not run out of beard cream he could leave behind a beautiful corpse with enough lush facial hair that the archaeologists of the future will be reduced to acts of necrophilia. Teddy did not mind anything as long as he was groomed to perfection. It did not matter that I was the only person around to look at him. I guess he wanted to impress the weeds and empty houses. It was a miracle we did not crash into anything on the way up here – he spent more time with his eyes on the mirror and less time on the road.

Dani Brown

I stepped around to the driver's side. Being outside of the car left me exposed to the weeds. They were of greater abundance in New Edge Hill than anywhere else. The low level blue glow had the effect of making them worse than their cousins closer to civilisation. The vines crept closer to me without moving.

Teddy stepped out of the car. He made no sign of noticing the weeds, not even a darting eye. He bent to check his beard in the side mirror, reaching into his pocket for the little container of beard cream stored there (Teddy Dick never went anywhere without beard cream in his pocket). The surprise I felt at him moving out of the way did not register until later. The weeds in their efforts to take control ensured it.

A loud noise shook the silence. The weeds recoiled yet stayed in the same places they were. Their hold over me loosened. The unease deep in the pit of my stomach did not leave.

Both car doors slammed shut on their own accord. I didn't like it; Teddy Dick did not seem to notice – not even when I could not get the doors open again. His beard was more important. There would be a comb lurking in his back pocket rich with grease. That'll come out last. The car doors had all the hallmarks of an invisible abduction from beyond the stars.

Welcome To New Edge Hill

We would need to proceed on foot. But I did not know where we would proceed to. If Teddy was to have his way, it would be in endless search of a Prohibition era barber shop. If I had my way, it would be somewhere away from weeds and invisible abduction (I did not want a probe).

The doors were unlocked; there was no logical reason why they would not open again. The vibrations from slamming shook the air like a bomb blast. I drew Teddy Dick's attention to it but he was more interested in shouting out. (All the noise would alert the aliens to our exact location.)

A detective should have been able to work out that we had obviously driven through some sort of portal, and we were now the only people – or someone flicked a switched and everyone apart from us disappeared. Or the weeds ate everyone. It did not matter what caused it (unless it was the weeds); the important thing was the loneliness, which only seemed skin deep. Something was out there (aliens obviously, the back of my mind chimed in). Some foe our colleagues did not know about before sending us to examine drone lights. Although they probably would have sent us even if they did know the sinister intentions behind whatever it was.

Dani Brown

I tried to recall whether Reptilian Shapeshifters from the centre of the galaxy appear with lights before stealing a human skin. I checked my phone, there still wasn't any signal to find out. Conspiracy theorists were never in agreement anyways.

The weeds were bewitched. And possibly a product of the Underworld. The eerie blue glow gave them away and presented the first line of enquiry. I did not want to be the one conducting it; we were sent to investigate lights in the sky. So far, I had yet to witness these lights.

The topic of the Underworld came up on occasion in the forums. The eerie blue glow was what sent my mind latching onto "Underworld" as oppose to alien. It was like everything festering away from my sleepless nights in front of the computer was coming at me all at once in the real world.

"Hey Teddy."

He looked over at me. He had the type of face buried beneath all that hair that I could not help but want to punch. My nails dug into my palm as I clenched my fist. Blood could attract the attention of the weeds. It was unwanted enough to relax.

"Shut the fuck up for a minute."

Under normal circumstances I'm a big fan of silence. But not when it is oppressive, yet sometimes when it is oppressive it needs to be investigated. I was not a big fan of Teddy Dick's shouting. On a normal day it would be the cause of a crippling headache – one that pain killers could not quite reach.

Teddy looked like I had punched him (I wish) rather than demand he close his mouth. The need to remain silent should have been obvious. He was a detective – curiosity and intuition were a given in that profession, but he did not express it in a very positive, proactive manner. It was a wonder he solved any cases at all with the way he behaved. I do not believe he was capable. His old partner would have propped him up. A simple statie with a sleep disorder could not do that – I wasn't capable, nor was it in my job description.

It was my turn to take the lead. My appearance would imply I was the one with half a brain but there were not any full length mirrors here. Never-the-less, I was conscious of the fact that even with no one around, I had a big, stupid looking smile plastered across my face. It was only a temporary thing – the weeds reminded me of their existence by doing nothing and wiped it from my face. A smile was my resting face.

Teddy Dick opened his mouth to speak. The glare I wore must have looked weird. It was enough to make him shut his mouth. His calls echoed off everything, leaving me unable to experience the silence I so desired and telling whatever was watching us our location (just follow the echoes for a tasty meal and enough facial hair to construct a stylish wig).

An unfelt breeze moved the branches of the trees creating a rain of golden rust-coloured pine needles. Unless the weeds sent invisible vines to shake them. The trees required more observation. Perhaps I would witness the glimmer of the choking weeds lurking within the invisible. They seemed to be in the grips of a slow death. Weeds were the only explanation my mind was willing to accept.

Not even in the boons do the leaves turn this early. Reds, yellows, oranges – there weren't all that many greens left, yet the diffused light still hit the blue glow of the weeds as green. If the trees were dead, the leaves would have been brown.

Whatever happened here was only a temporary thing. Nowhere along the roadside were the weeds shining in their own blue light. If solved and dealt with in the correct way it would not leave lasting consequences (I could hope). Then I looked over at Teddy, my heart now being swallowed by my stomach it had sunk so low.

That did not explain the pine needles though. I'm aware of evergreens shedding but this was sheer ridiculousness. The evergreens were going to be lost forever. A scout troop from closer to civilisation will come up here and plant new ones if it was safe to do so (and if the people ever returned).

Teddy Dick's footsteps sounded like a herd of angry elephants stampeding through the savannah on the soft earth; it appeared he had the intention to bang on doors. He carried his beard cream pot. I left him to it while I carried out the real detective work. He was knocking softly. Under normal circumstances it would not even be heard.

We should have turned around and started the long walk back to the station but curiosity was getting the better of me. As long as I was always aware of the weeds I would be safe to carry out an investigation - enough to at least ask more questions if not solve the case (these lights had failed to appear in the sky).

It was hard to say when the people had disappeared. Sometime while we were driving in search of Prohibition Era barber shops of questionable existence and mysterious lights in the sky. Our radio would cackle with life on any other day - it was silent since leaving the station. The people could have disappeared all at the same time sometime after we left the station or it could have been a gradual process - disappearing before we drove past their houses. That would not explain the weeds and dead radio. Maybe they reappeared after we were gone and the weeds interfered with the electronics (but my Game Boy still worked).

Nowhere had the tell-tale signs of a slaughter. Washing hung out on lines in back yards with more weeds than vegetables. They snaked up sheets still wet from the washing machine. The sheets lacked blood splatters and were covered in dust. I would have thought that the owners would have used the dryer instead of hanging them outside.

The possibility that the weeds swallowed entire families was one to be considered with the utmost seriousness. But the weeds were only glowing blue in New Edge Hill. They could not have sucked the others down to the Underworld without that blue glow.

Weeds are not capable of chewing, drooling out blood and spitting bones. Even these ones. They weren't big enough. With unfocused eyes they looked it, because they merged into one beating blue organism. Zooming in on one plant allowed them to be seen as they were; no larger than the weeds choking my flower beds.

With the car refusing to let us in, I decided the best course of action would be to investigate, being careful where I planted my feet least a dandelion reach up and grab me to pull me screaming into the Underworld. Even if that was not what happened to the people here, the weeds emitted an air of being more than capable. Rewards await whoever can suck the two cops down.

It was a long walk back to civilisation – walking back with Teddy Dick would make it even longer as I might need to fight him to prevent his running off in search of a Prohibition Era barbershop and beard cream store. Arriving back at the station, everyone will be having a laugh at our expense. They'll stop laughing when I describe the weeds. I should try to find a lonely sample so we'll be believed.

Perhaps someone in one of these houses will have their own hillbilly microbrewery. It did not seem likely that Teddy Dick would object to drinking on the job as long as the beer was obscure enough. It would give us a chance to learn to like one another. The circumstances called for it.

Everyone had left everything behind, including whatever they were cooking. Luckily it was too hot, even out here in the middle of nowhere, otherwise Teddy and I would have a lot of fires to put out, which was not our department or even in our job description. That did mean Teddy was not going to get his Salisbury steak and mashed potatoes any time soon.

The door on the first house was unlocked. Preppers and off-grid people had paranoia levels off the charts, so it seemed lucky the car did not boot us out in one of their villages. Their houses were like fortresses. They did not have bomb shelters through a secret door in the basement, because they're houses were defendable bomb shelters stocked to the brims with supplies and anti-government, anti-police propaganda.

Living in the foothills of the pathetic mountains, I must say I was expecting filth and photographs of generations of inbreeding. I was left disappointed in that regard. Everything seemed normal in the houses. Expect the crochet doilies. I hate doilies at the best of time but there were thousands in every house.

To live here, the requirements were a special type of patience and willingness to drive two hours to the nearest cereal café. A normal street bicycle would never be able to navigate the roads – to prove my point, I found a shed bursting with mountain bikes. Looking closer at the photographs I guessed the nearest hairdresser and barbershop were rather far away. And it seemed these people had not heard of beard cream, let alone experienced the wonders of such a product that kept their facial hair tame.

Even this far into the middle of nowhere, desires of normal pursuits were evident at every turn. There was even a home cinema and very decent sound system. The children had television sets and video game consoles in their bedrooms just like the children in the towns and cities had. Everything would have been normal if the people had pulled the weeds up.

There was nothing to explain the absence of the occupants. The other houses seemed much the same – sometimes the obvious pursuits of the people were different (instead of a sound system there was enough cooking equipment to run a bakery for the entire state). I stumbled across the doily maker and crochet hooks. If the river was nearby she (or he) could find them at the bottom of it but it wasn't so the yarns were safe.

It sounded like paper being torn in half, only loud enough for the vibrations to knock knick-knacks from the mantel. The ceilings were raised so when I jumped once it registered through the silence that I did not bang my head and knock myself out. A blessing, by my account at that point in time; upon reflection, it seems more of a curse now.

No one, apart from me was around to watch the knick-knacks shatter on the floor. Teddy Dick seemed more concerned with applying fresh beard cream from the supply in his pocket. (My beard had not come in full enough to require repeated applications.) He did not investigate the houses with me. Strange- he must have known there would have been larger mirrors inside.

I ran outside, back underneath the glare of the midday sun shining down on autumn colours despite the trees and the summer. It appeared Teddy did not look up at the sound. To me, it ripped across like the earth being torn in half. To Teddy, it probably helped style his beard.

I'm not sure he noticed me until I tapped him on the shoulder. He lost his cool and jumped yet still rubbed cream into his beard. His beard would have a sufficient water coating and enough oil to fuel a plane but applying more was ever so important.

"We need to investigate," I told him.

His jaw was as slack as what I imagined the residents of the houses had for their resting faces. The pictures on the walls were all portraits, leaving my old prejudices there beneath the surface to spew forth their hate – family albums with snap shots would prove me right or wrong but I lacked the time to look for them. Old prejudices were hard to kill anyways even with stacks of evidence reporting their falsehoods.

If the flies hadn't disappeared with the people then one would have flown into his mouth. Although beard cream was a good fly catcher. The weeds might be responsible for the disappearance of the flies and jealous of his beard cream that had the potential to kill many more than they could ever imagine.

The sound tore through the air again; louder without the insulation of the house. I desired diving under the car to get away. It stopped as suddenly as it begun. It was difficult to say what direction it had come from. It seemed to come from everywhere all at once and nowhere at all. I'm not sure if my ears were bleeding or wax was melting. If it was wax, I'm certain Teddy would have scooped it up for his beard.

High noon changed to midnight with less than a moment's notice as clouds (or not-clouds) rolled in. The sound was unlike thunder and according to my phone, none was forecast the last time I looked. I went to check it but all signal had magically disappeared. The clouds peeking from beyond the trees weren't rain clouds. The colour and texture were off. They were unlike any clouds I had ever seen yet Teddy Dick was more interested in ensuring there was not a hair out of place on his face. Staring at the sky could allow the weeds vital time to wrap a vine around my ankle and drag me to the Underworld.

The frustration I felt towards Teddy Dick was great enough at that point to show on my face beneath straggly bits of my attempts at growing a beard. As usual, he failed to notice. It was a vicious circle with increased frustration to follow

There weren't street lights at the base of the mountain. Some of the New Edge Hill residents seemed to have rigged up porch lights to come on at the first sign of dark. The lights were welcome even if they did not illuminate very much.

Either Teddy was finished applying beard cream or he could not do it by touch alone. He put the mini container in his pocket when the car door wouldn't open. It was the first time he realised we were locked out. In the shadows and covered in enough hair to resemble a well-groomed Bigfoot it was difficult to tell what he was expressing through facial features. Arms flailing about I assumed it was exasperation he wanted to communicate.

I was not afforded much time to study his face before an even louder crack rocked through the air. If I had suspected it was wax draining out of my ears before, it was now safe to declare it was blood. Teddy Dick would not want that for his beard. Travelling right to the centre of my brain it cradled something inside and not in a pleasant way either.

Something moved in the shadows, unless it was a trick of the flickering porch lights combined with my brain being violated in such a violent way. The trees could not project moving shadows and make leaves crunch underfoot – there wasn't any wind. It was possible vines sent up from the Underworld were strangling the trees and other plant life but the idea did not sit in my mind in the right way.

The sky above transformed into an eerie copy of high noon with blue and green instead of sunlight defused through the dying leaves. The reds, oranges and yellows did not change the quality of blue and grey. These lights could not be mistaken for drones. Movement made me check the ground for weeds too close to my ankles wanting a taste of my blood.

Teddy Dick pulled on the door handle – the car was not going to let him in no matter how well-groomed his beard was. The cream would make his journey to the Underworld easier with the extra lubrication if we did not find the things behind the shadows.

Something behind the houses moved as the thing in the shadows became closer. The abduction wasn't so invisible anymore. It was like something breathing down my neck but so far away. Warm air engulfed me for a moment before passing with no wind to carry it away.

Despite the eerie light, I could not make out what was lurking in the shadows. The possibility of a bear was entertained in my mind based on the way the residents kept their bins locked. But the bears disappeared with every other creature unless they were the only creatures left. Bears were wishful thinking reserved for people of a demeanour too positive to ever make it as a cop.

Dani Brown

Teddy Detective stumbled around with an air of nervousness, kicking dust into his freshly groomed beard to stick to the cream. The illusion of a Bigfoot was complete. I took the time to snap a picture – I would need to remember to upload it later when my phone found signal once again.

He mumbled, "I didn't sign up for this shit," beneath his breath on repeat.

Becoming a cop was a short cut to power which he did not get from his adoring fans with more hair on their beer guts than he had on his face. Beer gut hair lacked the careful grooming despite his attempts to throw beard cream and hair wax at them.

A third creature stumbled down the road. It was too scrawny to be a bear. Bigfoot with an eating disorder seemed more likely. Teddy kept up with his mumbling – I would have preferred a running commentary of what was happening.

The weeds curled towards the third creature. In the gloom it was impossible to tell if they wanted to suck it to the Underworld or worship it. They could prove allies if it was the former, yet, they could not be trusted.

My eyes darted around looking for an escape route. It seemed the unknown creatures had us surrounded and there was no chance of prey swooping down on them. At any rate, they seemed to be the largest animal in the foothills. Bears would only come out at night when the locals were snoring instead of sitting on their porches with shotguns.

The escape route had to be free of weeds. I would rather take my chances with the creatures than face the glowing blue plant life. The creatures offered my limbs being torn off; the plants offered the unknown suffocation and restraint of being dragged beneath the earth to the Underworld. As if the weeds could read my thoughts they waved. It lead me to believe they were winking at me (or I was losing my mind).

The creature lurched forward. It was still a ways off but its stumbling forward movements were a bit too quick for my liking. It was the spikes sticking out of the fur following the length of where I imagined the spine to be that really shook me up. The way the blue glow of the plants reflected off them and shone into my eyes with a sparkle was the most unnerving thing of all. I would rather an invisible abduction. Invisible abductions lacked spikes.

The fur was as patchy as my beard. It was hard to say if it grew like that naturally or if the creature had fallen into the weeds and it was torn out in the escape. I thought it might be a bit of both.

It dropped to all fours to run, which was still more of a lurching movement. Its tongue fell out of a long snout. It was like a dog – only the tongue was forked. Drool sizzled on the road implying it might very well be toxic.

Teddy mumbled. I expected him to squeal like a small child spying a giant mutant centipede. He was the type of person to pull wings off flies (at least as a small child but he still probably participated in the activity), he would not know what leg to go for first. He should have been giddy with the excitement of grooming the creature or plucking its fur.

Looking over at him I could see weeds snaking around his ankles. He did not notice the danger posed by the plants. It was the creature he mumbled at. Or himself – I could not tell. I assumed he was saying something different to before but I did not know, his words were muffled further by his beard. I pulled him back a few paces and the weeds withered, emitting brighter blue. It was all the confirmation my fears and suspicions required that the plant life was out to get us.

Plants weren't the only thing sent out to taste cop blood. There were the creatures and no rhyme or reason for this unless the force had trapped us in a virtual reality Hell. I did not believe that; they may have had jokes at our expense but this was too extreme.

Understanding of the creatures dawned as the weeds took on a hungrier vibe. They had spread to the mainland from Puerto Rico. I read all about them on cryptozoology forums. If these creatures had been let loose on the population there would be a river of blood. Dropped here from a different planet, before me lurched El Chupacarbas – that did not explain the weeds though, or lack of people and animals. I took my gun out. When dealing with something like El Chupacabra it was best to be armed unless one desired to end up disembowelled.

They behaved like a normal flea bitten dog, but even lacking intergalactic rabies, they were known for violence. A trail of dead farm animals followed their spread through the Americas. Other continents thought we were crazy with our guns but all they had to deal with was the Loch Ness monster and the occasional Yeti – Nessie could not survive outside of the water and Yeti were rare.

"Teddy, your gun."

Having to remind someone who was meant to be smarter than me felt more uncomfortable than having El Chupacabra running straight at me with more out there, lurking behind houses and trees, hiding in the shadows (I could hear them). Guns were no defence against flesh eating weeds though; only a strong weed killer would save us from them. Teddy did not even put on a display of reaching for it – a situation to increase my discomfort.

"Teddy," I shouted.

He needed to spend less time grooming himself and more time shooting at El Chupacarbas. It was unfortunate that on our person we only had force-issue hand guns. Shotguns were kept in the car – they were for taking out rabid wildlife and not SWAT Team activities (hey, that's why there was a stinking SWAT Team in the first damned place). Out in the boons, of which there were plenty in this side of the state, shotguns were a necessity. If the car had locked us out then it was reasonable to conclude we would not be granted permission to liberate shotguns from the truck.

"Teddy," I shouted again, my voice cracking with desperation.

His eyes appeared vacant. In all likelihood, his mind was at a Prohibition Era barber shop, playing Game Boy and listening to a cassette on his Walkman while he sipped microbrew and waited his turn in the squeaky old chair (not one to give him an electric shock, unfortunately, which might have returned him to the reality of our situation). Not bothering to put my gun away or even click the safety on, I shook him. Without my finger on the trigger it could not go off but with El Chupacarbas approaching that was a problem I wanted to remedy soon.

I needed Teddy, as much as I didn't like having to admit it. I needed another gun with a finger on the trigger and pair of eyes. The impression of him I had in my head was being replaced with that of a bumbling idiot who could not cope with pressure and who had sucked his way to detective. It was frustrating to say the least, especially in my time of need. He wasn't worth an alien parasite sucking out his brain through his beard.

The Force made jokes at our expense – a cop and a detective could not be partners even though we were constantly paired up, much to the amusement of the rest of the Force, town cops and even the Feds. Our opinions were always dismissed due to our beards, even mine in its patchy state and requirement of beard cream twice a day instead of twice an hour like Teddy Dick's. They'll accuse us of doctoring dashcam footage despite the lack of skills in the area of modern technology. They'll accuse us of attention seeking when they discover the complete lack of motivation for the crime. Suggestions of creative writing competitions will be hurled at us both while on desk duty like it is somehow our fault that the people who post on conspiracy theory and cryptozoology forums tend to be crazy. Even if we don't make it out alive, these opinions will be expressed at our funerals and be a talking source for years to come until it passes into legend.

I fired a shot. Even in the silence, it was not as loud as the sounds heard a few minutes earlier. I think I hit its knee but it lurched on with a trail of blood. The weeds lapped it up. Vines were sent for the creature – it always moved out of the way just in time.

Dani Brown

I fired again while Teddy Dick stood there on the gravel road, slack-jawed and useless. The better option for him would have been to deal with one of the other Chupacarbas or at least pay attention to where the weeds were in proximity to us.

My bullet, once again, appeared to have hit the lurching El Chupacabra. This time in the other knee. The temptation was there to pump him full of lead but my lack of extra bullets put me off going for over kill. The second shot slowed it enough for me to be confident it would bleed out and feed the weeds while I deal with the next one. At the time, my brain did not have time to process what the extra blood and tasty El Chupacabra flesh would do to the weeds.

The shots failed to wake Teddy from his stupor. At least he wasn't getting in the way but his help would have been more than welcome. Monitoring him and the weeds while knowing the location of the other Chupacabras required extra eyes and an extra brain – two things I could not pull from a pocket.

If need be, he probably would not have noticed if I borrowed his gun by ripping it out of the holster. As long as he did not think I was taking his beard cream – he would break my hand and perhaps my neck even.

The next nearest creature was darting through the woods, diving behind the trees in a clear display of intelligence. The other creatures may not have been

Chupacabras. My mind assumed they were because the first one in plain sight could be identified as such. If I did not learn to stop making such assumptions I would never advance through the Force.

My time spent in the dark web conspiracy and cryptozoology sites where the Feds could not go taught me El Chupacabra was like a vicious pet left behind by vacationers from the centre of the galaxy (usually of the Reptilian Shapeshifter variety). People held some strange beliefs in those hidden forums. The photographic evidence taken from numerous locations could not be disputed. It was technically possible they could all have been set up, faked and 'shopped.

El Chupacabra did not move with any obvious grace, giving me an advantage. They were loud and clumsy. There was now my own first-hand experience to add to the forums. Experience of a cop was worth more than that of a farmer, even though farmers had, overall, the more important job. Postings were mixed about the speed at which these things could move.

It was safe to assume they breathed heavily underneath all that fur. I doubted anyone anywhere had ever been this close to one. All the photos I had seen were obviously zoomed in – no one wanted to get close to them. It would be safe to assume their breath was lethal based on the way the drool smoked when it hit the ground.

They had more fur than Teddy Dick had face hair. The one lurching forward appeared in need of a haircut and a groomer – it was all matted together. That alone should have knocked Teddy out of his stupor and sent him scurrying with his comb and beard cream to give it a makeover.

There were still two out there – at least. My attention could not wander towards the finer points of El Chupacabra grooming. Teddy would probably give the creature a man-bun and that would be that if Teddy's mind was not lost somewhere where everyone had nice hair and moustaches creamed and twisted into spikes of death.

Surveying my immediate area: two El Chupacabras and lots of murderous weeds, one detective lost in Prohibition Era and not much ammunition. The situation was fucked but I was not granted the luxury of paying attention to such negativity. Man (and animals and now weeds) will fight to the death for the vaguest hint of survival.

There weren't any houses on the side of the street where second El Chupacabra was coming through the undergrowth. The undergrowth met the gravel and seemed intent on taking over running vines into the tire tracks. The houses could be out there with trees growing through the centre of them.

The weeds should have swallowed the creature whole and spat out his bones. The trees might have been choking them; they were losing the battle but the chances of losing the war were slim. El Chupacabra would not supply a clean shot despite its bulk and stumbling (I might be able to add poor eyesight to the forums but I would need confirmation).

"I require your assistance," I informed Teddy instead of shouting for help like a normal person.

Teddy Dick was more receptive of pretentiousness like the idiotic douchebag he was.

"Teddy."

Sweat coated my body. I could not recall a time when I had ever had so many emotions coursing through my veins at once. It was enough to drive me insane but I would have to process all of that later.

"This is Earth, calling Teddy. Come in Teddy."

El Chupacabra in the woods was creeping ever closer, not hindered by the weeds sent forth from the Underworld to claim souls. I spared a glance for the one with bullet wounds. It had moved towards us before collapsing in a pool of its blood (quickly being lapped up by the thirsty weeds to make them grow, but it would not satisfy their hunger). It was still too far away to tell if it had died while I tried to deal with its friend in the woods.

My back was turned to the third one; a position I did not like being in. Teddy Dick could have come in useful there – his delusions were more important it seemed. Wherever he was, it lacked El Chupacabras and weeds.

Drenched in sweat, my body still managed to make the hairs on the back of my neck stick up. My straggly beard was in a state rendering me grateful that I did not care about my appearance enough to check my reflection in the windshield. Asking to borrow Teddy Dick's beard cream may wake him from his stupor.

"Hey Teddy, lend me your beard cream a sec."

He stirred at that. Beard cream held more power over him than I initially suspected.

"El Chupacabra can't disembowel me and eat my entrails with my beard sticking up."

A very real possibility unless Teddy Dick came back to me. I did not want to be found with my insides on the outside with birds gnawing on them when the people return. I didn't care what my beard looked like as long as I made it out alive (and without an invisible anal probe).

"Beard cream, please."

I held out my hand and inserted a tone of pleading into my voice until it cracked with panic. If I could keep it to just my voice then I could convince Teddy Dick it was about beard cream and stand half a chance of bringing him back to reality. It was difficult to keep El Chupacabra from my mind, knowing they had some degree of intelligence, were creeping up through the woods and our backs were to the last (known) one beyond the houses.

To turn around and check on Chupacabra behind the houses would mean to lose sight of the one knowing the importance of discretion. Chupacabra behind the houses was loud and did not seem to mind who knew it was there.

"Teddy, I really need it."

The panic in my voice could be mistaken for whining which would further serve my purposes. Teddy Dick liked whining. It was easy to picture his wife using it to drag him away from the mirror and to bed.

"My beard Teddy, look at my beard, it no longer glistens."

The short hairs were standing up like the hairs on the back of my neck, both sets of human fur sparkling with the wrong type of glisten – sweat instead of cream. His eyes burrowed into me as I tried to track El Chupacabra. Movement from him was better than his slack jawed stare. And less creepy. I could only pray he shut his mouth. It wasn't like there were flies around to

Dani Brown

land in it but I did not appreciate the views of his dental work and who knows what the weeds could send up from the Underworld to land on his tongue and lay eggs. To look over at him, even for a brief quarter of a second would mean missing my potential shot.

El Chupacabra was closer now, lurking in the undergrowth before the trees. Without the trees shielding it there was a higher chance of hitting it but the undergrowth was thick.

El Chupacabra did not make any noises, not even when they lay dying and weeds lapped up their blood. They were heavy enough to hear them crashing through the surroundings which had alerted me to these three. Another silent enemy; it did not do much to help my levels of anxiety. An invisible belt tightened across my chest. Inhaling deeply I was able to shake it away. Luckily the only smell to greet my nostrils was Teddy's beard cream. The invisible belt was a gift from my own mind, not even invisible aliens were that good.

There was a third known Chupacabra lurking behind the houses. The possibility of one sneaking up on me and Teddy occurred. These three were obviously male – females were lighter on their feet. A shudder ran through me. I had to tame it to aim the gun.

At closer range with a perfectly timed shot I may be able to blow this one's brains out to splatter against the trees and mystify the residents (if they ever return).

Welcome To New Edge Hill

Unless weeds eat splattered brains too. El Chupacabra dropped to his belly. I watched him pull himself along. That must have been a thick hide beneath the fur to withstand the brambles.

In slow motion El Chupacabra stood up offering me a clear shot to its head. My arm was already up, supported by the other, aiming for an eye. My arms protested. The invisible belt around my chest tightened itself but not as tight this time – I could deal with it after I make the shot. If I didn't make this shot pieces of me and Teddy would be wrapped into a singular body bag because only DNA testing would be able to tell us apart (provided people reappeared from wherever they'd disappeared to).

The creature had an odour of rotten eggs and fermented melon. It was overpowering enough for me to have to consciously fight my feet from taking a step back (Teddy's beard cream was not strong enough to mask it). I could see the flare of its nostrils and the red flecks in its eyes. Never in my life did I imagine I would be this close to El Chupacabra – the guys and the girls in the forums will be impressed. And it was all in the line of duty.

My sweat made the trigger slip beneath my trembling finger. The gun slipped from my grasp, or maybe it was my imagination, or the will of whatever

Gods govern the Boons. The gun went off. The bullet hung stationary in mid-air, plainly visible.

Time for El Chupacabra did not move in slow motion – movement for it was the up and down of inhalations and exhalations, the slight flare of its nostrils. Smelling that bad, it was amazing it did not knock itself out by breathing in the pungent odour.

The bullet slowly started moving towards the target. Even in slow motion, it was impossible for me to tell if it would hit or miss. It was not worth a look at the weeds. My attention needed to be on the bullet. I'd grabbed the gun and was ready to fire another.

El Chupacabra did not seem to notice the small object racing towards it but the creature moved around a lot in its quest to disembowel us (and probably its companions as well). It could move or duck its head or stand before the bullet reached it.

My lungs threatened to explode from a breath I did not realise I was holding. Slow release just does not happen in slow motion. It forced it out of me until I gasped for the next inhalation resulting in a temporary loss of the bullet.

It entered through El Chupacabras head. Being so dark I did not realise until I saw brains, blood and bone fragments explode into the trees. El Chupacabra continued moving forward with time restored to a normal pace. I thought I might need to fire another bullet. At this point, it was missing at least one fourth of its head, yet, it clawed its way forward through the undergrowth and met the first roadside weeds with its finger tips.

I was surprised to find the gun still in my hand. I repositioned it. Before I could fire and waste a bullet, the creature realised it was dead and keeled over, draped onto a low hanging branch. Nerves kept it twitching. As fascinating sight; I would have loved to watch but I had Teddy Dick to bring back to reality from wherever he was zoning and a third Chupacabra to kill. I needed to check on the weeds progress as well – I did not want to kill three Chupacabras only to be overpowered by weeds and sucked down to the Underworld.

With the world moving at normal speed I could not risk leaving my back to the third Chupacabra for any longer unless I fancied having my entrails torn out through my rear – a situation I wanted to avoid. Turning around, I spared a glance at the weeds. The blood was powering them to a growth spurt. It would have to be dealt with after El Chupacabra.

I would have thought the sound of repeated gunshots at close range would have been enough to bring Teddy back but apparently not. I hoped it would not come to running over my Game Boy in front of him (provided the car wanted to let us in). I could not bring him back to the station in a stupor —a short cut to the monotony of desk duty. Stealing his beard cream might prove the most effective. It would not require pleading with the car either. Beard cream would allow me to style El Chupacabra's fur, snap a photo and upload it with so many hashtags all the world will see (except the residents of caves lacking entirely in signal). But first I had to kill the remaining Chupacabra.

Apart from Teddy's shallow breathing, El Chupacabras movements were the only sounds to be heard. The way they echoed off the trees and houses…it would be less creepy if they howled or growled or made some sort of noise with their throat. I was confident it was echoes and not a fourth Chupacabra. I could not feel another pair of eyes on me. Female Chupacabras were probably lighter on their feet but I would know if one was amongst the weeds.

A fourth, like the first and second, would create its own distinct rustling with its own distinct echoes. In the silence, sounds held extreme significance and they were easy to tell apart. Beneath El Chupacabra there was the continuous drone of the weeds' groans as they grew and took on more power. Being a musician afforded me keener hearing than most but I'm sure even someone non-musically inclined would have heard the weeds.

Turning around was a painful endeavour due to my hips sending sharp pains both up and down. The invisible belt of anxiety seemed to have grown spikes and attached to my feet. I suppose that was a good enough place for it while I took care of the last Chupacabra. The effort to move produced more sweat; it did not lubricate the anxiety away. If I make it out of this, the rest of the force will never let me live it down. Constant cans of antiperspirant – reminders of my humiliation – would be better than being disembowelled through my anus I reasoned.

I had my drum kit and Teddy Dick had his wife and kids to return home to. I had to see us both out of this alive – she had affection for him, as did his children. It was not them who had questionable intelligence and a job they were quite frankly, too stupid for. By that point I had given up on him standing next to me and shooting his gun.

If being less than twenty-four inches away from me burrowing his eyes through my flesh and raping my soul while I fired bullets into a sneaky beast from the centre of the galaxy was not enough to shake him back to reality before I steal his beard cream then shouting his name stood no chance. Teddy Dick was useless; the soul-rape made me question his usefulness in other aspects of his life in the back of his mind. Perhaps, in death, he would be more useful to his wife and kids?

Dani Brown

But I wanted to have a 'later', and live in a world filled with people and animals. There needed to be a 'later' in which to deal with the pain of recoil from a pathetic force-issue handgun ripping through my body. A 'later' in which to come down from the anxiety. A 'later' I could use to brag to the people behind the screennames on the forums undetected by the Feds (they would laugh and laugh if they found out why I had been losing sleep).

I was not fond of firing my gun – this might be the last time. With a shot timed and aimed to perfection there would be no need to take it out again (I could hope). A gun would be no use against the weeds unless it magically started shooting weed spray.

I bit down on my lip, sending blood into my straggly beard (instead of beard cream), to find the strength to face the creature behind me. It stood there on two legs staring me down. Cryptozoology and conspiracy theory forums were never clear on whether El Chupacabra walked on all fours or two legs – I guess it was a combination, like bears. Not like it mattered when one was staring you down looking for the best place in which to run its claws along your abdomen or turning you over to reach into your anus for those precious intestines.

Its small frame bore no relation to the size of the claws – completely out of proportion compared to the rest of it. There were not any farm animals around to eat – there were no farm animals in the foothills (unless the odd family kept a pet goat or pig – some people do).

There weren't even any flies to buzz around the rest of the animal El Chupacabra did not eat. El Chupacabras only liked to dine on intestines as far as internet cryptozoology and conspiracy theory forums were concerned. There were the weeds though – the weeds had no problem lapping up blood. They were probably chewing on fur right now to get to the bones of the Chupacabra in the middle of the road.

There was only me and Teddy Dick to eat. We would provide miles of intestines for the one lurking behind the houses. As El Chupacabra had no issue eating chickens, I doubt they would find two granola-eating Staties too small a meal. The granola would make our intestines extra tasty – premium sausages to wash down after all those fast food fed entrails they sometimes dined on when they could not find a farm. After us, El Chupacabra might be reduced to consuming leaves – they weren't known for a vegetarian diet.

I fired. The world did not slow down this time. My trigger finger was in the beginning stages of developing a cramp which would wake me in the middle of the night for years to come. El Chupacabra raised his head and howled in silence (on reflection, I do not believe they had vocal cords). He was hit.

He fell to all fours sending a cloud of dust from the gravel into the air. Weeds sent vines to his wrists and ankles – either another meal or one still enough alive to pull to the Underworld. He tried to fight, stirring up more dust and attracting more weeds looking for a cheap meal (or victim).

With the last of my failing finger strength I pulled the trigger again – a weak Chupacabra was still a hungry Chupacabra. The bullet shattered through the vine of a crawling weeds before hitting the wrist. The weed sent pieces into the air before shrivelling and emitting a final flash of bright blue light.

I do not know how much time passed. I watched until El Chupacabra breathed his last. The weeds claimed him. Wrapping their vines over his corpse and disappearing into a hole in the Earth. Blue fog rolled out of it in thick clouds before dispersing at ankle level. It was cold enough against my sweat-stained skin to remind me there was still danger out there.

Sunlight, defused through autumn leaves, was restored. Obviously they weren't, but the leaves seemed a bit greener and more alive. Oppressive silence beat down upon the trees and the weeds groaned at ground level. I could not write it off as a bad dream; not with a dead Chupacabra and blood-thirsty weeds littering hillbilly country.

Something was absent. The penetration of my soul by Teddy's eyes. Looking around I discovered him sat in the driver's seat. At some point while I was watching the weeds engulf El Chupacabra things started to return to normal. It would be a gradual process. My desire to be out of there did not overrule my need for understanding (or requirement of a shower before people returned). The weeds still thrived in their blue light. If things were returning to normal, they would be sent back to the Underworld. They may try to drag us both down with them in a last ditch effort to impress whoever ruled them.

There was lots to do before total normality could be restored. I was confident it would be – I could feel it creeping in as the blue glow of the weeds flickered and died. People returning from where they had been would not want to see the corpse of El Chupacabra splattered across their overgrowth; it may further distress them.

El Chupacabra needed to be dissected. There was one body left. The weeds had the other two – something that I still consider to be a blessing. The weeds would not get the third. Apart from losing their strength, I would not allow them the access. Farmers needed to know what they were up against before the government buried the corpse and me and Teddy with them on red herring conspiracy sites ("Something happened but we're going to point you delusional people in a different direction!").

It was hard to say whether Teddy was back in reality or not. He was, once again, attending to his beard. Although beard grooming was important, I did not believe it was vital. His assistance would help him return to reality and remain grounded there but I doubt I would get it. It was not worth the stress of asking.

I wanted to drag the dead Chupacabra to the car. It could be delivered to a person I know. The perfect person to perform the autopsy and let us know what we were up against should more of the creatures be left on the planet. She was as mistrustful as the government and Men in Black as anyone else I knew but worked in a hospital morgue, giving her access to the equipment needed as well as the knowledge.

In an ideal world, I would be able to fit El Chupacabra in the car. I would have the strength to move him without breaking into a sweat. But the car was small and cops were notoriously out of shape. It had to be the one in the undergrowth that was not claimed by the weeds. Bramble appeared to have snagged its fur – the splattered blood and brains could be blamed on poachers so at least I would be spared the ordeal of scraping that up. Although I did not indulge in the doughnuts my peers used as their main diet, I was partial to whatever eight hundred calorie seasonal latte or iced latte was the special in the various franchised coffee houses that tried to put the doughnut shops out of business. My belly jiggled; it wanted more latte over ice and would laugh as I struggled.

Even if Teddy was back in reality he would be of no help. Teddy Dick was the type of person who didn't like to get his hands dirty. My subsequent sigh was loud enough to turn his head. I was stiff and sore – the least he could have done was put some cushioning beneath my head while I was passed out watching the weeds but his beard was more important (obviously).

Bits of gravel clung to my straggly beard. A weed crept too close to me and snuggled next to my ankle. I stepped on it with my heavy Force-issued boots. The crunch bounced in the silence. I rubbed my foot along to ensure it was good and dead – like a smoker with a cigarette butt in forest fire territory. The bottom of my shoe was covered in smoking blue goo.

Gravel combined with sweat to tangle my hair. The only relief was to be found in the shower creating a dilemma in my mind; there was no-one around to prevent me using the facilities in a house but I did not know when they would return. The weeds still had an air of blueness surrounding them implying I had long enough to move El Chupacabra to the trunk and wash the sweat off me in the shower before anyone knew me and Teddy Dick were there.

It was vital I had El Chupacabra stowed away before the people discovered us. El Chupacabra would be sent to a government lab and buried in the most unbelievable of conspiracy theory and cryptozoology websites. I could not allow that to happen; the people had the right to know but not like this, it would freak the hillbillies out.

My muscles protested at the thought of liberating a fur-covered body from the brambles that held it so close in death's embrace. At the thought of dragging it to the car they held me in the threat of imminent crippling cramps. Teddy Dick might as well have not been there for all the use he was. I wanted this day to be done and over with – I planned on giving my drum kit a miss and crawling straight into bed with several heating pads.

"Better to get it done and over with," I told my muscles. Then, if no one suddenly appears I can have my shower. I promised the muscles lots of boiling water and a nice massaging loofah dripping with the most luxurious soap the hillbillies had on offer. It made them obey my commands. If people do return, I'm sure no one would begrudge a cop some hot water, even if they happened to be uber-paranoid and fond of off-grid living, as fellow human beings they would help me out.

Welcome To New Edge Hill

The weeds did not win against the undergrowth and trees regardless of how hard they tried. But it was the few that tried I had to watch out for. They were desperate for a prize to take back to the Underworld – even my boot would do. They bled green where the brambles stabbed them. The blue fog was thicker in the undergrowth but it was sick, dying even, with splotches of grey.

A few weed vines snaked into El Chupacabra's fur looking for entrance into his body – a feast before they're called back to the Underworld. I had to go back to the car for a knife. Teddy seemed unconcerned and went back to grooming himself, leaving me to wonder if he desired a quick fuck with a hillbilly woman before returning home to his wife.

The weeds had not made any progress in anything except the act of dying. That could prove the most lethal time. I went straight at them with the knife. If I was to succeed I would have to throw caution to the wind and be quick. The caution joined the anxiety to be processed later, possibly with the help of some super-strength medication (provided I could get a prescription).

The brambles fought me along with the weeds. They weren't sentient though so it could not be down to some defence of their cousins from the Underworld.

Dani Brown

They were just bastards the locals should have taken a machete to ten years ago. They probably made pies from the berries which made them reluctant to do so.

I would need a new uniform after my battle with the brambles. I did not look back at Teddy Dick sat in the car – I pictured him snickering at me as he applied more and more beard cream (the glove compartment was fully stocked).

A weed caught my finger. The fucker stung worse than the thorns. Spikes entered my blood stream via a small cut. I was not sure whether it was toxic or not. It was unlikely Teddy Dick would bother to put down his beard cream long enough to help and get his manicured fingers dirty so I did not shout out for assistance and raise my stress levels. It would only prove a distraction and minimise my chances of freeing myself.

Toxins from one weed was not enough to immobilise me but it was enough to cause pain. The interruption gave it precious seconds to alert its friends to my weakness; seconds were all that was required. More vines crept out of nowhere, most leaking green blood into the blue fog as I killed the one latched onto my finger. That many vines would cripple me.

The trick was to not allow them to touch me. I grabbed a bramble – the kiss of a thorn was less painful than the kiss of death. I wrapped it around my non-knife wielding hand and arm to fend them off. Some cowered away. They would not have their prize to take back to the Underworld and show off in hopes of a promotion.

The fog thinned out. The blue was fading. I was grateful but knew it signified I might not have much more time before the people and animals returned. It also gave me the opportunity to see what I was doing properly. It should make the operation run with more speed provided my muscles believed the promise of a skin-scorching shower afterwards and the strongest painkillers in my medicine cabinet when I return home.

Tugging on El Chupacabra would do no good until I removed the worst of the brambles. My muscles would not like me very much if I tried. I choked back anxiety – shaking would only make the task harder. Each thorn attached to a bramble needed to be lifted with care and patience so it would not get caught in more fur, and then discarded.

The fog faded further while I was busy. Looking around after I was done, there were only a few remote patches of it left. The age of the weeds was finished. The relief I felt was soon chased away by anxiety – I did not have much time left and I really needed to get in a shower.

El Chupacabra was heavier than expected. He needed to be dragged, being careful not to tangle him in anymore brambles. It was unfortunate that I only had half his head and his brains were splattered on the trees (making them smoke). We could learn a lot from the creature's head. The lack of it did not make him any lighter. I was not thinking when I was shooting with two of the creature's charging at me. If the Force get wind of this and my trigger happy fingers I'll be put on desk duty where they can tease me relentlessly.

My back was howling by the time I pulled El Chupacabra to the trunk. The least Teddy Dick could have done was open it when he saw me close by. I asked three times before walking to his open door and doing it myself. I somehow resisted the temptation to have an accident involving my elbow and his face. His beard would have protected him from any bruising. It would need to be re-combed though with fresh cream. I did not have the patience for that sort of thing.

Popping the trunk took half a minute away from destination; shower. It was so close I could taste soap bubbles in my nostrils. But not close enough – if the people return before El Chupacabra is out of sight I would have a lot of explaining to do in passing it off as a bear with suspected rabies.

I did all the hard work, becoming sweaty and dusty in the process, while Teddy Dick sat there grooming himself. It was rather insulting; insulting enough to result in pictures of him stuck to my drums for the banging I intended on giving them the following day (provided my muscles would allow it). Resentment bubbled away inside me – I did not swallow it down with the anxiety and pain but allowed it to fester.

It was lifting El Chupacabra to the car that presented the issues in terms of time consumption – trying to work muscles that don't usually see that much attention. The resentment created tensions and knots in them that would need to be massaged out. Try as I might, it could not be swallowed and dealt with later in a constructive fashion – Teddy had gone too far.

Teddy should give me a massage but that might give him the wrong impression if I was to ask (and make his wife jealous in the process). He had better lend me some beard cream after my shower. If he really wants my forgiveness, he'll act as my barber and apply it while giving my straggly hairs a little trim and comb. Even if new partners could be found for us, I had the impression we were going to be stuck together until retirement.

Lugging the corpse up to the half way point was difficult enough without thoughts of Teddy shining my boots and trimming my beard until I was the one to impress the ladies. I vowed that I would work out every morning and cut back on the seasonal high calorie coffee drinks if my muscles would just cooperate. The promise of a shower should have been enough for them but it wasn't.

Blood matted El Chupacabra's fur. It still smoked from where the weeds had dripped into it. I would be sitting in the passenger's seat naked unless the hillbillies had spare clothes in my size. My uniform needed a date with a BBQ and bottle of lighter fluid they were so badly contaminated. To deal with my resentment I imagined the squeal of the microbes as I threw a lit match on top of my trousers.

The smell was enough to make me wish I had allowed the weeds to take me. I did not bother to count how many times I swallowed down vomit and burning stomach acid. I'm sure the guys and gals who worked homicide would claim to have me beaten. They had never smelt El Chupacabra – blood drenched crime scenes had nothing on that odour. Breathing through my mouth stopped the scent from hitting my nostrils with the full force but I did not like the thought of intergalactic bacteria and parasites entering any part of my body.

Due to the heaviness of the creature it was hard not to nuzzle its fur. I looked up at the sky to spy the trees returning to green but nearly dropped him. At least I was able to get a few breaths of fresh air in. Even hillbillies use mouthwash in this day and age – especially with the nearest dentist being a two hour drive away. If I could not find any, I would take a bottle of their strongest alcoholic beverage and wash my mouth out that way. But first, I had to get El Chupacabra in the trunk.

I thought the legs would be lighter but I was sorely mistaken. My arms could have been tired but I really do think the legs were heavier than the torso. It would have been pointless to try and work out why. The pathologist could work it out when she slices him open and tell me why.

There was no way Teddy Dick could have missed the sounds of me struggling. He choose to ignore me in favour of his beard cream, despite there being no one around to impress with facial hair groomed to perfection. Even if there were people around, they would not have been the type Teddy would have wanted to impress. He wanted girls with Game Boys and bad taste in music.

He should not have wanted anybody, his wife was hot and as sweet as a cinnamon roll. She kept him in supplies of beard cream and guitar strings. She gave him a foot rub after his shift despite the fact he did not actually do much of anything apart from groom himself. I would not be the one to tell her this though.

My clothes were stuck to my body with sweat by the time I had the body loaded into the trunk. For every inch of clothing, there was at least one hole. I was bleeding from just about every part of my body. The cuts weren't deep enough to lose enough blood to pass out though.

My state of mind was detached, like I was watching it all play out on the silver screen with a sepia tint by this point. Mentally, I had yet to deal with the disappearance of people, animals and insects – for at that point in time, I viewed it as normal, something that could be dealt with later and added it to the sepia tint my mind assigned to the lifting of El Chupacabra. Resentment, fear and anxiety become lost and confused in the sepia.

I don't recall thinking it had been a dream; the festering corpse of El Chupacabra confirmed everything had, in actual fact, happened. The lingering weeds from the Underworld waved at me in an attempt to fracture my mind beyond repair. Although the last patches of fog shone in sepia, I knew they were blue.

It would have been outright delightful to say a nightmare resulted in such bad sweats my bed linen had to be changed in the middle of the night. I wished I could say I experienced a brief break with reality. But with the glassy eyes and matted fur staring back at me, those privileges were denied.

The rest of my time spent in New Edge Hill (I later confirmed that that's where we were) passed in a sepia tinted daze. I have trouble recalling what happened and in what order. The flashbacks and nightmares come to haunt me but I can't be certain it happened that way.

Two shallow graves were found by officers looking for me and Teddy Detective. The weeds had buried the other two. They were found without their limbs. Apparently the trip to the Underworld was made piece by piece. They weren't afforded enough time here to take the entire creatures despite their numbers.

There was no Prohibition Era barber shop and beard cream store – it had all been a prank. There weren't even any funny lights reported in the sky. The other officers just made it up one night over beers and doughnuts because they were bored. They were not to know that there were actual lights.

The bodies were evidence that screamed that something had happened. Remnants of dead weeds that did not return to the Underworld were bagged up and sent for testing. Their origin could not be confirmed even upon resurrection in a secret government lab (so secret most of the government was not aware of its existence).

When we did not return, rookies were sent to bring us back. They drove straight through New Edge Hill (there was only one road through the village) twice before they crashed into the car and the residents re-appeared as if they had not been missing. According to reports, it all happened at once. It could have been me and Teddy who went missing from reality and brought back dead El Chupacabras and flesh hungry weeds.

Such a mess was left in a bathroom that had an occupant sat on the toilet reading the news on a tablet computer and the imprint of the toilet on his backside, implying he had been there for at least twenty minutes. He claimed he was sat there for an hour. His wife and children backed him up – all stating they had banged on the door to get him to hurry up at least once.

He never saw me in there as I never saw him. The bathroom was vacant when I went in for my shower, even in sepia. The towels were light and fluffy despite what my vision told me. And the loofah was oh-so scratchy my muscles forgave me. I felt good. Refreshed. Everything still played out in sepia. In my mind, those images now have black spots littering them but I can recall the texture of the loofah and the relief it brought as if it was yesterday and everything was normal.

The rookies questioned my towel use – it took three to dry myself off, all with hairs stuck in them. I remember that. It threatened my detachment. To come crashing back to reality all at once would send me straight through to full-blown Looneyville never to return.

Some lab, not sure which one, later confirmed they all belonged to me and came out of my beard. Had it been shown to come from my pubic region, embarrassment would have been an understatement, but in all honesty, I thought beard hair and pubic hair were the same. I chucked the results into a drawer where Teddy Dick could not stumble upon them.

The residents of New Edge Hill were normal folks who preferred the isolation of the foothills – nearly as high as the pathetic mountains they surrounded. Hillbilly had been my technical term but they were all former city folk. The house foundations in the woods were from a settlement over two hundred years old. They re-founded the village, rechristening it "New". They wanted to raise their children closer to nature and away from the stresses and population of the city.

They were more than a little freaked out when me, Teddy Dick and a trunkful of dead El Chupacabra appeared parked in the middle of the road only to be crashed into within a few seconds by the rookies. New Edge Hill had more investigators descend on it than the residents had ever seen – despite one member of the community having previously lived next door to a crackhouse. This I confirmed with a few questions while

I walked around without much of a clue as to how I got there and nothing to do except figure out what happened and try to place everything in a logical order in my mind as a big 'fuck you' to the sepia and black spots.

Teddy Dick sat in the driver's seat with his beard cream – it did not matter to him that his door was now embedded in the front of the other cop car. He felt the car shake with the impact though. It would have been hard to miss while grooming. It was not until later, when everything had died down and the creatures were confirmed to be El Chupacabra that he confided in me that excessive application of beard cream was how he dealt with stress. We were beginning to confide in each other – the start of what might be a wonderful and long partnership (if I can learn to ignore his womanising). Not like we had any say in the matter, we were stuck together for life now.

He claimed he had a fancy beard long before they were fashionable and promised to show me pictures to prove it when the rest of our belongings arrive. He even suggested we start a band together while we wandered the gardens trying to deal with our trauma before our new job begins.

We were taken to the same place El Chupacabras and the weeds were in black unmarked vehicles. I suppose they could have been dark blue but my mind wants to replace the sepia with black as that's what I've grown used to seeing around here. We were both given unlimited access to anywhere we wanted to go on the base. Even me with my conspiracy theory history. I was the only one to look for the answers. Teddy dealt with his trauma in an entirely different way to me.

I found the pathologist conducting the autopsies on El Chupacabras. She had been looking for me. She wanted an explanation about the missing limbs – if things had played out the way I planned, my friend would have never enquired. It was difficult to describe the weeds. They had burned themselves onto my memory in colour but the words weren't there.

She gowned me up. The biohazard suits weren't necessary as far as I was concerned. I had already been exposed to intergalactic bacteria and parasites but the military were more paranoid than their conspiracy theory counterparts. They scanned me and Teddy Dick for any and every possible disease before allowing us out of isolation.

Everyone confirmed El Chupacabra were dead – heck one of them had its brains blown out. They were kept in deep freeze for a week while Teddy and I were in isolation. Nothing except resurrecting microbes could survive that.

Dani Brown

The pathologist claimed all three began to twitch at the same time. I was not paying much attention – chasing sepia thoughts in my mind instead, even though an autopsy of the creatures could prove more enlightening and help me place all the pieces together in my brain (and return the memories to colour).

I was standing next to her. I failed to notice the first twitchings. Maybe I thought it was normal. I read something about nerves living past the deceased. I thought maybe deep freeze had done something to stop post-mortem twitching. I did not understand the significance of what was happening.

Once I realised that what was happening should not have been happening, I was grateful I did not take El Chupacabra to the woman I knew and the other two had been discovered. Once that relief washed through me I was able to swallow the rest of my feelings and sepia tints to spring into action. The pathologist did not scream. Neither did I. I think Teddy would have.

The door was not locked. If it was, I would have broken out. The entire military complex lacked locks. Security was hidden. I could only hope they were watching. Shouting in this place would do no good. We would not be able to hold it for long.

The pathologist stood clutching a scalpel and shaking with a vacant stare when I next looked over at her. She would be needing treatment after this. I grabbed her by the wrist on my way out of the room. She did not need to see the reanimation. Not even scientific curiosity made me want to stay in that room. I could always watch the video playback later if I really wanted.

My Force-issued gun had been removed when Teddy and I arrived. Lest we decide to go insane (I don't really think anyone actually *decides* to lose their mind), we had yet to be issued with new, more powerful weapons. We were still under observation and could not even be trained in usage yet. It did not stop me from reaching for it though – even though it was obvious the bullets would not keep the creatures dead.

She was shaking, yet her body hair did not seem to be standing up – electricity did not cause it then, just my body's reaction. Running out of the room with her, I wrapped my arm around her shoulder. We could feel the electricity from the reanimation in the air. The beginnings of panic reached me when I could not get the door to close behind us. I swallowed it down and discovered it was her foot in the way. Tightening my arm around her shoulder, I manoeuvred her out of the way.

The parts of the base I had been escorted around were apparent with their lack of locking doors. No one told me there weren't any but I just assumed. Not even my apartment had a lock on the door. I suppose we were meant to trust each other. We were all former police officers and military personnel who had stumbled across something we weren't meant to see, forming this secret section of the military. Right now, a lock would have given help an extra minute or two to arrive. I was new. I did not know it would not take them long.

I expected locks everywhere and to have to beg for a pass in a place that was meant to be as secure as a secret military base when me and Teddy Dick were informed of our new role in the world. The location I did not know.

All sorts of things were undertaken to ensure my complete confusion upon arrival. When me and Teddy were first bundled into the car with blindfolds and blacked out windows for good measure, I thought we were being driven away to be killed. I've wasted too much time in my life on those conspiracy theory websites. It made me paranoid and untrusting.

There was a door between myself and the three El Chupacabras but one without a lock. I shouted for assistance. Good old conspiracy theory paranoia and trust issues had kicked in. They would dominate my time under observation and make it stretch longer than it did for most.

Despite her shaking, the pathologist was of much more use than Teddy Dick was in my sepia-tinted nightmares and flashbacks. The old resentment started to bubble again – it had the potential to destroy the start of a beautiful friendship and partnership.

She went away. She left me to hold the door shut by myself. No wonder I had trust issues. It did not matter that in less than a minute she had returned with two heavily armed guards. The anxiety was there and it would not go away. Not until I was back in my apartment with a high dose of Valium. The pathologist was still shaking; I assumed her plans for the evening (or was it morning) would be the same as mine.

I had both hands on the door handle but due to intense sweat I found myself losing my grip. Then I heard their footsteps. The room beyond was meant to be soundproof but the racket of reanimating space animals echoed down the corridor. The armed guards went in without saying a word to each other. They were much calmer than I was. I wondered when observation would end and training would begin so I could be that cool under pressure too.

The sound of gunshots greeted my ears; someone had skimped on the sound proofing. When no one knows of your existence, there is no one to complain to about funding cuts. The armed guards ran out and slammed the door again a few seconds later, pale and shaking and out of ammunition. The funding cuts were worse than I imagined.

Dani Brown

The banging behind the door continued. The only thing worse than three Chupacabra running loose on a secret military base was three Chupacarbas capable of spontaneous reanimation running loose on a secret military base staffed by survivors of paranormal events in serious need of a nerve tonic. Before vacating the room with the shaking pathologist, I did not think to check if the two with missing limbs had been able to regrow them. It would not surprise me if they could. Nothing could surprise me anymore. That did not mean it could not make the anxiety build a tight invisible belt around my chest.

I resumed my position holding the door handle. Anxiety could be dealt with later. In fact, it could be added to the large stack of stuff my brain had yet to process and return to colour. I set my brain to work thinking of a way out of this predicament.

El Chupacabras capable of reanimation would need to be killed in a special sort of way. If the requirement to study them for understanding, science and defence was now defunct, then a flame thrower would prove useful. It might be the only option.

Years of crappy B-movies as well as Hollywood lied to me in regards to reanimation being due to the brain. One of the reanimated creatures was missing half its head and had a severed spinal column. Unless it only required a few lingering brain cells. Most of that creature's grey matter was left behind in New Edge Hill smoking through a tree.

As it was, a guillotine would have been helpful – provided I could lure them to place their necks on the block with their last shred of dignity and it could cut through the spikes following the length of its spinal cord. Somehow I doubted El Chupacabras cared about dignity. There was always the question of whether or not it would work. It was easy to picture them – two of them with regrown arms - grabbing their heads and lurching towards us.

An axe might prove more useful – I could chop them into itty-bitty pieces. Tiny pieces had less chance of regrouping. It would present time before they could regrow missing pieces from the tiny parts. It could create a lot more El Chupacabras to break out of the base and wreak havoc on farms up and down the Americas, hitching a lift on a ship heading towards the Old World until a worldwide famine is declared and they have to survive on the flesh of starving humans. Time to find a way to ultimately destroy them before that happened would have to be found.

Even a secret military complex should have a fire axe somewhere (or weapons capable of chopping and poking). They were probably stored behind the only locked door in the complex.

Dani Brown

I could not very well stand here gripping the door handle as sweat made it slippery all day. My trip to New Edge Hill seemed to have damaged my sweat glands, I had been sweating since being driven out of that place in a blind fold. The two armed guards and pathologist lacked the nerves to be employed by the military. But this was a secret military of survivors. It made the collective a bit nervous and scatty.

I doubted a fourth person would have been any better but maybe, if they did not see the reanimated Chupacabras they could hold the door shut while I went to find a weapon. I did not trust their nerves to find a weapon and bring it back. If my future was to be jumping at my own shadow, I wish my initial suspicion of being driven out of New Edge Hill in an unmarked car to be killed had turned out to be true.

I went into a striking rendition of various snippets of grunge songs in my tone deaf voice (and sounded like I would make a decent grunge vocalist if I ever became bored of drumming) to draw attention to our plight. It was the first thing to come to mind. Shouting for help would not result in it. People here were too nervous and scared. Easier to hide behind unlocked doors and hope for the best.

Shouting for help would do no good when the secret military base seemed to be populated by personnel in need of nerve tonic. It might send the rest of the people here into a state of panic behind their unlocked doors and alert El Chupacabras to their existence and the tasty intestines beneath the flesh. Looking at the three people surrounding me, I grabbed the one shaking the least and had him hold the door handle. I left the pathologist in his care and as back up while I grabbed the other in hopes he would calm down enough to help me find a weapon and way to eliminate the reanimated El Chupacabra.

The military base was set up like a maze. It would not surprise me if genetically engineered rats were wandering around the empty corridors somewhere deep underground, forgotten by the scientists who created them. Giant rats weren't my concern and I hoped they never would be. I made a mental note to never leave food out in my apartment for their genetically enhanced sense of smell to find and gnaw with their giant genetically enhanced front teeth.

"We need a weapon."

The solider next me waved his gun lost for words. I rolled my eyes at him. It was hard to believe that even in panic someone was so stupid and incapable of independent thought. I'm guessing he must have been from one of the more disposable military units who witnessed paranormal activity and were now doomed to spend their rest of their miserable post-traumatic lives guarding a secret base.

"Not a gun – something that can cut or chop with a long handle. An axe maybe?"

He looked lost. He must have been able to think with that much clarity at least, otherwise he would not have survived this long.

"An axe? Surely you have something other than guns in this vast place."

The way my voice bounced down the corridor was not reassuring. It caused a flashback to the disappearance of all living things in New Edge Hill. I did not have time for flashbacks right there. I seemed to be the only person who did not require an immediate tranquiliser direct to the blood stream. Issues of psychology were not my strong point so I allowed the flashback to run its few second course and hoped the rest would run around in the back of my mind until I could deal with them.

The man looked clueless. There was too much light in the corridor shining from overhead. The tiles were too white, as were the walls. I preferred the sepia tint of New Edge Hill. The weeds with their blue fog that burned through it were less terrifying than the white and reanimated El Chupacabras.

It would be too easy to get lost – I lacked a trail of bread crumbs to drop but I'm sure my beard shedding will serve; dark fibres on the cold white. It would have to do. The stress and anxiety had been making it fall out. Teddy's beard tonics did nothing to restore it but I could not bring myself to shave.

No sound came from behind the numerous doors we passed. I could not be certain they were weed-free because samples of those were scooped up from New Edge Hill and goodness-knows where else. They were dead when they were bagged and labelled but as El Chupacabras proved –things do not stay dead.

"We need to defend ourselves."

A spot of drool seeped down his lips and caught the bright white light of above, sending a rainbow onto the wall. The only colour in the place. Even our clothes were white. The echoes were creeping me out. I gave up trying to talk to him. I would never get any sense out of him. A smell greeted my nostrils; it was not bad enough to be El Chupacabra escaped from the room but it was still pretty bad. He would leave a brown trail for us to follow back – I had that to be thankful for at least. One positive in a white-washed sea of negativity.

Next door I made a decision to open it and look inside. A whole new world lay in there. Humidity punched me in the face and wrapped around my beads of sweat. Blue fog fell out of the room. Someone in white was breeding these things I wanted to leave behind in New Edge Hill.

The soldier next to me made me long for Teddy Dick and his beard cream. His nervous reaction was better than the soldier's blank stare. He stayed back in his apartment next to mine when I invited him along. He longed for his wife and the warm parts between her legs. She was not allowed in. His family had been moved to a variant of the witness protection programme to ensure they could handle it. They were told he died in the line of duty and for reasons of secrecy there could be no funeral. He mourned the loss of his children's sticky chocolate covered kisses. Not enough time had passed to convince him getting out of his apartment would take his mind from it.

A vine curled around my ankle. They remembered me. That was not my post-traumatic mind thinking either. These things remembered what my blood tasted like. They wanted to send more green goo into me and cripple me to take me piece by piece back to the Underworld. I could only hope the scientist running this particular operation had thought to cut them off from it prior to resurrection. Everyone here was so nervous, I'm pretty confident it was taken care of.

I shook my foot free before anymore could come out and shut the door. They all looked the same but I determined not to open that particular one again by only opening doors beyond it rather than random darting. I hated weeds. The hatred was entirely rational after my ordeal in New Edge Hill. I was not too fond of things that were blue either.

The corridor went on for miles – I could not see the end or any turnings. I knew there were stairs, I had descended a few flights on my way to the morgue. The miles of white seemed to add to the confusion and maze-like feeling, even though a straight line was not part of any maze I had ever known.

The door next to the weed room offered another corridor that went on forever with doors all the same. I had two choices: turn around and shut the door or go down it and risk losing myself. I would never find the door leading to this corridor again in amongst all those other doors – I had nothing to mark it with, nothing that could be used as a weapon. Even my beard scissors, which could have carved a big X into the door, were taken upon my entry into the military labs. Teddy had refused to give up his beard scissors and stayed in his apartment mourning his old life; I knew there was more too it but I had my own problems to deal with so would only ever allow myself to scratch the surface of other people.

The guard standing next to me might not like the indignity of having his backside wiped against the white door but it was the best I could do. I did not want to stumble across the weeds again. I was confident another door would lead to another corridor further up. It would allow him vital time to regain his nerves. With them he might have a better idea but without them, he would not put up any resistance towards me using his smelly accident as a door marker.

I opened the next door. I closed the door. I did not want to go in there. I don't know why. It was some sort of intuition telling me to stay away despite it being a small white room with no furnishings. It lacked any purpose except to act as an empty room until it could be filled with mops, buckets and brooms or paranormal experiments.

There would be something to keep my bearings while I could turn around and see two dots in the distance which were the pathologist and other soldier. They were quickly becoming smaller. It seemed we had gone a mile down the white corridor without accomplishing anything except discovering the resurrected weeds behind a door somewhere between here and the reanimated El Chupacabras.

The next door offered a glimpse into nothing. It was literal nothing. The void. To walk into it would not mean death but it would not mean life either, or even suspended animation. It gave me the chills. I slammed it shut – the nervous wreck of a soldier beside me jumped and leaked into his underwear a bit more with a soggy one. At least he had reactions, more than what could be said of Teddy once he was applying his beard cream. I missed him though. I thought of him back in his apartment applying beard cream in front of the mirror until it was water proof.

I skipped a few doors before opening another. Secret military bases offered up the weird. That was for sure. Especially ones entirely staffed by people who had traumatic experiences with the paranormal while in the line of duty.

Lurking behind this door I finally found what I was seeking. Axes, swords, throwing knives. All of these might prove useful against reanimated Chupacabras. There were not any flame throwers though; I had a feeling it might come down to that. If El Chupacabra missing most of its head could come back, I wasn't sure what knife wounds would do. They might be dead for a little while but come back hours or even days later seeking entrails. A short term solution would afford me time to think. I grabbed all that I could carry and instructed the soldier beside me to do the same – he may have been a nervous wreck but years of training insured he was capable of following directions to the bitter end (even with his own raw sewage lining his white trousers).

Dani Brown

We ran back to the others. The dots became blurry shapes before they took focus. I was careful not to slip on the shit trail the guard left for us to follow back. With the other two still vaguely visible we did not need it.

We arrived just in time to hopefully save the day (or night – time lost meaning here). El Chupacabra had a clawed hand sticking out of the door frame. A matted brown in a sea of white. It looked new. It could have been paranoia but I think it meant these creatures could regrow their body parts.

The pathologist had vomited all over the white tiles. It splashed on the white trousers of her plastic biohazard suit. I did not want to live a life where I was so nervous and anxious I would lose control over my body functions.

There were no injuries. Had we explored another room, we would have come back to discover these two disembowelled and three Chupacabras (one re-growing half its head while shards of brain-coated bone stuck to its spine spikes) running lose. I did not know how many people worked behind these doors. The death toll could have been high.

I dropped everything except an axe and cut off the fingers sticking out. A loud cry was muffled by the shitty sound proofing as the door slammed shut. Vocal cords had obviously regenerated while in deep freeze.

Welcome To New Edge Hill

Crashing to Earth to be left behind by their Reptilian Shapeshifting owners made them lose their voices. I almost felt a twinge of empathy at their abandonment here. That could prove fatal despite its promise to restore my mind. There would be time for empathy later –when lives weren't in danger.

The creatures could feel pain – that was good. That was something positive to focus on. El Chupacabras making sounds while I inflicted it was not so good though. I had feelings. I did not like to hurt things, even if they were animals from another planet more ill-tempered than an overheated raccoon with rabies.

The pathologist and two soldiers were huddled together shaking beneath the bright lights. Vomit and diarrhoea splashed the uniforms of the soldiers. Vomit decorated the pathologist's biohazard suit – if she lost her bowels as well I would not know.

At least two of them could follow explicit directions. I was not sure about the woman. She worked for the military but there was no way of knowing if her training was as much a fundamental part of her as the two soldiers. She did not tell me what her job was prior to her placement here. I guessed it was part of a medical team but that did not mean battlefield medic.

Muffled bangs and high pitch noises (possibly the creatures communicating with each other for the first time since being left behind on a strange planet) escaped the bad sound proofing. I cursed the fund cutting.

Footsteps, many footsteps, echoed off the tiles. I turned around. At least twenty soldiers were jogging towards us, all heavily armed and wearing white uniforms. Relief washed through me until I realised all they had were guns. Guns were no use against Chupacabras capable of reanimation. It was like being trapped in a bubble when I tried to explain. The words would not come out and I was pushed to the side to watch as they entered the morgue. El Chupacabras would not die.

The muffled gun shots did not cease to echo upon reaching the door and walls of the room. The noise created was bad enough to send my lunch back up – I swallowed it back down, lest any end up in my straggly beard. A shower did not seem to be a likely possibility any time soon. If I impressed whoever was in charge by not losing my lunch I could be taken off observation and placed onto active duty. It would be better for my mind than spending my days wandering aimlessly and my nightmares haunted by visions of New Edge Hill. I had steadier nerves than anyone I met here anyways.

My imagination ran away to distract what the sounds were doing to my physical body. I tried to keep it in beard ointment territory and away from anything that could trigger a deluge of bad memories. Perhaps excessive automatic fire from twenty guns might be enough to ensure El Chupacabras could not come back. My imagination did not like the gunfire despite it being different to that of my Force-issue hand gun. Each round fired I heard, even though the guns were automatic. They came at me, one after the other; memories flashing before me before I could recognise what they were.

The soldiers never left the room, unless they went through a different door (this place had far too many doors). From the other direction, a door shut and there were more footsteps – fewer this time. People in white suits had come to escort me, the two soldiers and the pathologist away from the door. I jabbered about gunfire not being enough to kill El Chupacabras. I did not think they were listening. I told them that to take out something that has spontaneously reanimated a flame thrower was required.

I guess I was relieved that they were there to rescue me. I did not sound relieved at the rescue though. My jabbering was heard as nervousness. I was becoming one of them. I would break soon. They had to listen to me about El Chupacabras. They said it would be taken care of. I would have to trust them. They had dealt with a zombie outbreak not so long ago – they knew what they were doing. These were not soldiers from the base but soldiers stationed far away who could teleport in to deal with problems. They were once nervous cowering wrecks as well.

I wanted to be out of this place. Despite my time spent lurking on internet conspiracy and cryptozoology websites I did not experience any serious fear before New Edge Hill. Well, it would be more true to say, I had no experience of fear that did not have a perfect base in reality. I always assumed I would be allowed to leave. I heard others in the housing complex talking about trips to the beach and whores in the city. I wanted to go on a long walk. I knew I would not be granted permission while under observation but surely not losing my lunch counted as something. I would return once my head was clear. I pleaded with them. They did not respond.

The handlers of the special secret military had ways of clearing heads. They were becoming more effective all the time. I was informed that the people on the base were working on the base because they were still too nervous to be sent out into the world. The clear headed soldiers who teleported in were used for more serious matters. I was still getting my head around teleportation being possible.

The room I was lead to had Teddy applying beard cream in front of a mirror. His wife held her face in her hands – sobs escaped her. The children slept with the dog on the floor. His family were here. I don't know when they brought in but it must have been while I was in lab complex. They must have finally revealed to her that Teddy was not dead. But despite his longed-for family there in the room with him, Teddy did not stop grooming himself.

I hugged her close. If Teddy would not give her the attention she needed I was more than happy too. Her grief was an odour that clung to her. I wanted to wash it all away. I wanted to smash Teddy Dick's mirror on top of his groomed-to-perfection head.

Teddy eventually put down the mirror. As expected, his beard was waterproof. It was only then that he came for his sobbing wife. He was worse than the people who would not answer the door while in their pyjamas no matter how early the bell rang, but take the time to get dressed and made up first. I left them to it.

The apartments had colour. We were allowed to decorate however we wanted. Although funds weren't unlimited, the budget was more money than I had ever seen before – part of the healing process. The base promised they could repair fractured minds. Teddy's hot wife being here was part of it. When she was done brightening up their apartment I intended on employing her skills in mine. The previous tenant of mine had preference for dull colours but even that was better than

Dani Brown

the white of the lab complex. It did not offer warm hugs though. I needed warm hugs to repair my mind.

For now, I could enjoy the warm embrace of a hot shower. The steam might chase the flashbacks away but it might not. We shall see.

Me and Teddy have become the conspiracy.

~Dani Brown August 2015

Welcome To New Edge Hill

~More from MorbidbookS on Kindle hyperlink image above~

More from *The Queen Of Filth!* An excerpt from Dani Brown's *"Middle Age Rae of Fucking Sunshine"*:

Rae, her buck-tooth grin and rosy cheeks of middle age acne reflected winter sun. Straw-like blonde hair obscured by the veil and tiara she enjoyed parading around in. She walked past our window with sickening confidence oblivious to us and our weak tea.

Rae. Everything was always about Rae. Was she a princess today, or was she a bride? Did she know or care? Did it even matter? We wished we could be that delusional and walk around with an air of not giving a damn...

"Middle Age RAE of Fucking Sunshine"

ONE

Rae never realised marriage is for life and not just for two weeks. She also never realised grown women shouldn't play dress up or not in public at least. That sort of thing should be saved for the bedroom and cos-play conventions.

Rae is the reason why the rest of us aren't allowed to make that life-long commitment. Her actions made the rest of us too stupid to understand the meaning of marriage regardless of how high our I.Qs might be. We know exactly what marriage entails. It is a commitment some of us are desperate to have but we will never know the joys of walking down the aisle.

Some of us had our children taken away because Rae drowned her offspring in bleach, piss and after-birth. We would have never done something so evil and sick. Some of us choose not to reproduce so we wouldn't learn the heartache of having children taken at birth naked and covered in blood. Rae's children were never taken away; even after she drowned the first two within minutes of pushing them out.

Rae. None of us have a job because of her. We exist on welfare payments and charity. No one wants to give someone who had a traumatic start to life a job in case they go bat-shit crazy. They think we might lock everyone in a parking garage and seal up all the vents, except the one used to pump in cyanide gas and wait for someone to try to ram the barricaded doors as people switch on their cars and the cyanide mixes with exhaust. Society thinks the rest of us will do that. Even after the unfortunate fume-filled demise of her colleagues that she watched on CCTV, Rae was able to find a new job. She kept her job after she posted the footage online with detailed plans of how she was going to repeat it on her new colleagues.

Instead of filling our days with meaningful work we fill our days with weak tea and the support group for those whose lives have been so thoroughly destroyed by Rae there are no longer any pieces to pick up. They've been shattered to dust. Nothing can help us now. Not even Rae's death would help, although that would be nice, especially if it was slow and painful beyond all description.

We sit around and talk about ways to convince society and the authorities and pretty much everyone that none of us are anything like Rae the Super Life Destroying Villianairess with a little touch of rat (at least on her face). No one ever believes us no matter how much we put into our efforts. We have to give more of ourselves to each thing we do due to abuse from so long ago as it is without Rae and her antics making all former victims (the press's words) come across as damaged goods.

Rae has stacked up more two week marriages than the mutants in the forest have fingers and toes to count them on. But her marriages affect them too. Due to Rae, the mutants in the forest don't have their marriages recognised by the government. In some cases, husband and wife are separated by the state just because they have extra fingers and toes and forked tongues and live in the trees. Rae has never lived in a tree; princesses don't like trees unless there are MDF castles in them, but those in authority don't care.

She is known to social services yet Rae can continue destroying everyone's life in a ripple, like throwing a stone into still water. Even people who have never met her and don't even know of her existence have their lives ruined by her.

We ladies in our support group can't live life as we choose. We can't do anything except sit around and drink weak tea with UHT milk. Some think we shouldn't be trusted with the kettle and mugs. They vow to take them off us. We would tell them where they can stick the kettle and mugs but we had our toaster taken away last year when some social worker who never met any of us decided that one or more of us might stick a fork in it (we're only allowed plastic sporks and it has always been that way). The paranoia of losing our tea is very real. It is, rather literally, all we have left – even the clothes on our backs are in the process of disintegration and we don't know when we'll be allowed new ones.

Rae is the local jiz-recycling plant. Society thinks every other person who has been at the receiving end of a violent sexual assault is always interested in more. Most of us here in the support group can testify that statement is false but no one listens to us. On the rare occasion when someone does, the absolute opposite of what we say is recorded.

Last week Sally won a trip to the cinema from the radio station. She was taken in the toilets by three of the employees. This week she has to sit on one of those inflatable doughnut cushions popular with haemorrhoid suffers. Rae is a giant bleeding haemorrhoid blocking the anus of our lives but there is no doughnut ring cushion to make sitting down any less painful. Sally has the underlying smell of stale popcorn about her still, underneath the combined odours of piss and shit.

We've reached the end of our tolerance of doing nothing except sitting around in our support group drinking weak tea and exchanging medications and Rae-related horror stories. We're going to do something about Rae. It is about the only thing we can do to benefit humanity.

Dani Brown

We've had enough of being told we don't know what marriage means because our lives bore some slight resemblance to Rae's or we had one thing in common with her – notice the past tense. It is always the past and never the present or the future. In our support group it is the distant past of our miserable existences. But the authorities and society don't care. Once you've been bathed in Rae's filth there is no bleach strong enough to cleanse it away.

Rae shouldn't be allowed to continue in her existence. None of us would hurt our children but we aren't allowed to know their post-adoptive names. Or even the area of the country they are living in. It isn't our fault Rae took the decision to drown everything she has ever let fall out of her gaping vagina (there was no pushing involved there).

We've been pushed too far by Rae and the people who agree to marry her with the belief that this time she has changed and the nuptials will last beyond two weeks. She is never going to change. She doesn't have it in her. And she doesn't think she does anything wrong; it is everyone else with the problem.

She has left behind a trail of very broken people (and drowned infants and gassed colleagues). All those husbands and wives and their partners before she snatched them away in the ripples of devastation.

Welcome To New Edge Hill

More than one of her spouses had a child or two from a previous relationship that she drowned in her pool (compensation payment). Every life those children touched has now been destroyed. How Rae and her spouse were awarded custody instead of the child's other parent is beyond our comprehension, especially with her record of murdering children.

All those families she broke apart when she gassed her work colleagues with cyanide and exhaust fumes. She carried on as if nothing was wrong without a care for the children of those people she killed or their partners, parents or twenty cats. Everyone had someone in their lives, no matter how miserable, which cared about them – now they're left tending gravesides and shedding their pointless tears into urns.

Rae had this need to cause drama wherever she goes. Her constant desire to be the centre of attention causes those who bear witness or worse, involved in one way or another a mountain of trauma that lasts for many years if they're lucky enough to make it out alive. Without the drama of other people's wrecked lives she will die from malnourishment.

Let's not forget about us in our support group with our weak tea. We take little sips and complain about all the negative ways Rae impacted our lives until it is time to go back to our dilapidated homes. We repeat every weekday, except bank holidays. We've done it every weekday for years. We have nothing else to do and nowhere else to go.

Every now and then a new member joins. Sometimes the new member had her life recently ruined by Rae but often times she had her life destroyed years ago and only now found out about us by wandering into the community centre during bad weather. We aren't publicised, but then again, neither is the International Sheep Hoarders Association North West England and Northern Wales Branch (they meet in the community centre too).

The younger members never last long. They don't believe their lives are forever ruined. They try to pick up the pieces. Too many fall through their fingers because Rae gave them proverbial carpal tunnel. They try again and again until all the pieces have dissolved into dust and blown away on a Rae-scented wind ripe with an airborne mutation of the herpes virus.

TWO

We're going to take action, once we decide what that action is going to be. Rae can't continue to wreak havoc where-ever she spreads her legs. It comes down to us. We're the only people who really know what Rae is capable of. It is rather obvious all the bad in the world has her stink on it but the people remain oblivious.

Welcome To New Edge Hill

Sally thinks we should violate her anus with a razor wire wrapped cricket bat. The support group shot this suggestion down; Rae's anus holds the world's record for loosest; she wouldn't feel a cricket bat even if we put razor wire dipped in chilli oil around it. We'll let Sally have a cricket bat and razor wire so she can relieve her anger and have her vengeance for the cinema incident.

We require an idea that will make her suffer. It should take away parts of her soul, over a shorter timespan than how we were separated from ours. It needs to always be a reminder of us and our weak tea. We aren't allowed the types of films, books and games where we could draw influence. Weak tea isn't the best creativity or intellect driver but some arsehole thought it a good idea to make LSD illegal. If this butt-wipe knew of Rae, LSD would be available from the supermarket right next to children's cough formula and sniper rifles.

Debbie suggested we kidnap her. Once Rae is in our custody we should drug to make her more docile. That's the next logical step. Between us we're on enough meds to open a small chemist. But we don't want her too docile; she might not realise anything is happening to her and that would be pure insanity on our part. Contrary to popular belief, we aren't insane.

Dani Brown

Lisa thinks if we hold Rae's head in a tank of pedicure fish with flexi-straws shoved up her nostrils it will be like waterboarding but with fish acting like the prize in a box of cereal. She spewed the suggestion out quickly with much mumbling. It took a few moments for it to translate in our heads. It showed such brilliance from one who hardly spoke at all. We would have been curious to know what else Lisa keeps behind those sunken eyes of her's but the excessive meds clouded our thoughts and we required all our brain power to form a plan.

We agreed that Rae's wrists and ankles required binding for successful waterboarding. The festering water could make the drugs wear off and she is a beast of a troll-like woman with the strength to overpower any of us with ease.

We should use the rusty razor wire that Lucy stole from the industrial estate two weeks ago. We need to put it to use before someone discovers it and takes it away. The kleptomaniacs might steal it and hold it to ransom. But it isn't them taking it that we're worried about. If someone in authority finds it, we may lose our weak tea forever.

With the basic formation of a plan we needed a fish tank filled with little flesh eating fishes. We weren't allowed pets. We were deemed too immature to be entrusted with keeping something else alive. None of our

Welcome To New Edge Hill

homes even had the most basic of potted plants because, apparently, plants have feelings too.

Not so long ago, even the high-end spa-style nail salons offered fish pedicures in their windows. A tacky High Street nail bar in an area with high unemployment should have at least one fish tank filled with little fish that feast on dead skin straight off the bloated feet of customers. There are at least five of them in the town centre alone.

It has been said that anything unfortunate enough to fall from Rae's vagina was drowned a short while later by its mother. Maybe the sensation of being held under water will result in a sudden attack of conscious (unlikely) or post-traumatic stress (we can only hope). If the faces of her murdered infants flash before her eyes and she bursts into tears she might be heard so we should gag her with Sally's crusty underpants.

Sally liked the idea. Her lacy pound shop panties were splattered with blood and pus and smelled strongly of urine and shit because it hurt to wipe with the cheap scratchy toilet paper provided by the community centre. She didn't have enough spare change to buy more than three pairs of pants and she was only allowed to do laundry once every other Wednesday so she wore her underpants for days at a time.

Sally was in no condition to aide in the theft of a fish tank. She stayed behind to ensure there would be plenty of weak tea upon our return. It pained her to walk and it pained her to sit down but she had those teas waiting for us. She even found a pack of biscuits. They were a bit soft but it didn't matter. Biscuits in any state of freshness were a rare luxury. Some of us hadn't tasted them since our lives were good.

THREE

We put the fish tank in the middle of our weak tea room without spilling anymore festering water down ourselves. The other support groups didn't offer their assistance. The choice they made instead, to gawk as we struggled past their rooms was typical of the apathy of lives destroyed or controlled by one aspect.

A lot of water spilled when we lifted it out of the nail salon. That meant the tiles in the salon were slippery and we left a trail of water down the High Street but the floor in the community centre remained dry – that was the important thing. Any sign of non-conforming and we'd be labelled as even more damaged and could lose our privilege to the community centre.

Fish tanks are heavy, made more so, due to our weakened state from poor diet. The dead and dying fish didn't have much weight but the water did, until we spilled most of it leaving the salon.

Welcome To New Edge Hill

The kleptomaniacs have jugs in their treasure chest of stolen goodies. We had no doubt that if we asked one would be made available for our usage with no questions and we were right. We didn't really want to add fresh water but we didn't want any more fish to die. They needed to be alive to swim into Rae's ear canals.

We took the tank with an ease that surprised us all. For once, something seemed to be going in our favour. Life was never that easy for any of us. We were anxious about when the theft would catch up to us.

It was opening hours for the salon so the doors were unlocked but no one was inside and the lights weren't on. The lack of customers and staff didn't become curious until we returned to the community centre. But not curious enough to waste precious brain power contemplating. Our brain power was needed in trying to decide what to do next.

Edie used to keep fish in ponds and tanks before Rae wrecked her life. She said that without any filtration the fish would suffocate in their own filth. We knew we would have to kidnap Rae before the fish could perish. At the nail bar it wasn't hooked up to any pumps or filtration devices. The creatures were probably seen as disposable to the salon as other peoples' lives are to Rae.

Dani Brown

The cleaners were addicted to heroin; they would never notice the fish tank – they were only trusted with watered down cheap disinfectant (which they probably still tried to get a buzz from). We were only left with hope that no one of importance would peek through the re-enforced glass window of our door. Our weak tea was at risk. We sweated with the knowledge but something had to be done about Rae. No one less damaged was doing anything about her.

We wouldn't be damaged if Rae didn't exist. Society awarded us the label, we didn't consent to it. Rae is the damaged one. In turn, Rae damaged us but not beyond repair until the authorities got a hold of us. They said the word, "broken" and took away everything we had worked towards and held dear.

Tomorrow we will track down Rae for a date with the fishes (before they all die). We have a general idea of her movements. We don't stalk her exactly, but it is always a good idea to keep track of the one who ruined a life or many lives before they can strike again.

After our final cups of weak tea we filed into the toilets – both male and female because there aren't any men in our support group and we're always the last one to leave the community centre each evening. The recovering chocoholics leave half an hour before us. They have pleasant homes with nice families and pets and chocolate stashed beneath the floorboards to get back to.

Sally cried out with enough pain to shake the cold air strong with the scent of watered down disinfectant and cheap air freshener. The sound was more like a cat being gang-banged by much larger cats than something from a woman's throat. Urine burnt when it hit torn and battered skin. She passed around pictures of her injuries so each and every one of us knew what urine and shit were splashing against. It was amazing waste could pass the purple swelling.

The doctors gave her the minimum of treatments. The event was a name a lifestyle choice by the nurses and hospital social worker. They said she was over-reacting. They sent her for a psychological evaluation when she denied it and asked for better treatment with some painkillers. She was threatened with being struck off for asking for a second opinion. She couldn't even walk the day after her trip to the cinema. We had to do our best to carry her to the community centre when Debbie found her passed out on the pavement. We all went home with sore backs that night. None of us bothered seeing a doctor as apparently our backs didn't hurt; we were simply seeking attention and wasting time.

Dani Brown

Once we finished we switched off the lights and locked the door, like we do every evening. The community centre actually trusts us with a set of keys, which is really kind of them. Not many people trust damaged goods with anything. It is a big responsibility and the only one we have. We share it.

Sally took the keys home with her. Letting her have the keys since the unfortunate incident in the cinema has given her a sense of purpose and reason to live, especially as the police refused to take a statement believing she was up for it regardless of how many times she said she wasn't. How they drew such a conclusion is beyond our reasoning. We suspect they might be both lazy and stupid.

End Excerpt.

Welcome To New Edge Hill

Dani Brown is the author of "My Lovely Wife" and "Middle Age Rae of Fucking Sunshine" (both out now from Morbidbooks). When she isn't writing she enjoys knitting and thinking of the finer points of invading Finland with an army of chavs mounted on dingoes. She has an unhealthy obsession with Mayhem's drummer and doesn't trust anyone who claims Velvet Underground as their favourite band.

~Maybe it had started when he was at university. He had a girlfriend in his final year that had gotten him into some weird stuff sexually then she left him for a guy with a bigger cock. The other guy was some gay looking chump with muscles and a tattoo; the pair had died in a car accident and Brian took a dump on their graves after each of their funerals. Fuck the both of them. But after she had left him he needed to fill the void of the newfound enjoyment of sickening sexual practices. Brain had purchased one of those 'real life' sex dolls online. Boy did the thing look real; you could bend it into any position and it came armed with enormous tits, willing mouth and a supposedly real feel pussy and anus. The packaging said to 'just add lubricant' but there was a problem. There was something missing; the smells, the tastes and the feel of real skin. You can't emulate that. So Brian set out to attempt to build a real life sex toy made from real life people.

~Keegan is a late-night public access radio show host, sexual deviant, and militant vegan. He has grown tired of his vegan cause being treated with apathy by the portly, meat-gorging, residents of the small town of Breen Gay, Wisconsin. The time is ripe for Vegan vengeance. Keegan harvests roundworms from a local vagrant and mutates them using chemicals stolen from the meat packing plant. He infests the populace with the voracious, parasitic carnivores. Keegan knows that the only way for the people of Breen Gay to eliminate the parasites is to starve them of meat. It is with great expectation that he awaits the oncoming utopia of Veganism. However, the mutant roundworms will not die easily. The problems for the people of Breen Gay have only just begun.

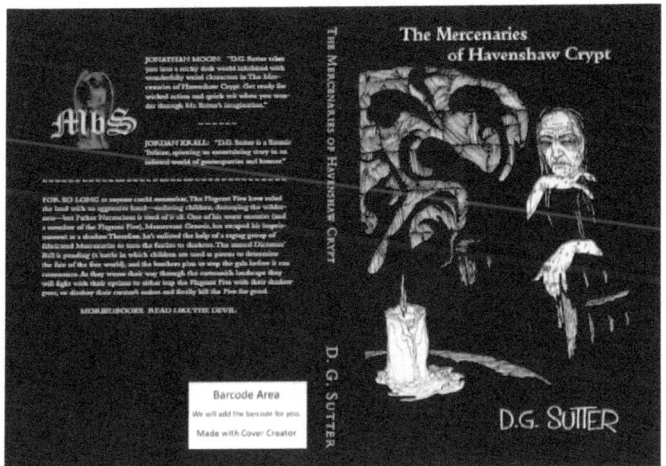

~FOR SO LONG as anyone could remember, The Flagrant Five have ruled the land with an aggressive hand—enslaving children, destroying the wilderness—but Father Necrocious is tired of it all. One of his worst enemies (and a member of the Flagrant Five), Manservant Genesis, has escaped his imprisonment as a shadow. Therefore, he's enlisted the help of a ragtag group of fabricated Mercenaries to turn the fascists to shadows. The annual Dictators' Ball is pending (a battle in which children are used as pawns to determine the fate of the free world), and the brothers plan to stop the gala before it can commence. As they weave their way through the cartoonish landscape they will fight with their options to either trap the Flagrant Five with their shadow guns, or disobey their creator's orders and finally kill the Five for good.

~The hands of the girls were inside of each-others zip front grey boiler suits and they sat in the blood from where Sonny's face collided with the surface. The brunette had a finger smear of it next to her mouth.

"You two sluts put each other down and go tell Moira that Sonny's done. I'm coming in, just got a little business to attend to first."

As the two started to leave the big blond grabbed the shoulder of the red head and pulled her back.

"Not you Fire-Crotch, all this fucking blood has got me going." She started to unbuckle the belt on her camouflage hot pants. "Down you go, bitch!"

~**Short stories from the Most Depraved Writer in Print.** Dark and twisted tales of exquisite violence, rough tricks, narcotics consumption, evil ghosts and drug-snuffling demons. Evil grandfathers and animal-human hybrid clones. Morbid serial killer stalking night darkened hallways of an unsuspecting hospital. Life underground following the frozen apocalypse. Tales of ancient blood-thirsty vampires and Roman decadence. Enjoy all of the hardcore, dystopic, viscerally violent stories. Not for easily offended mamby-pambies. Dark fiction at its finest.

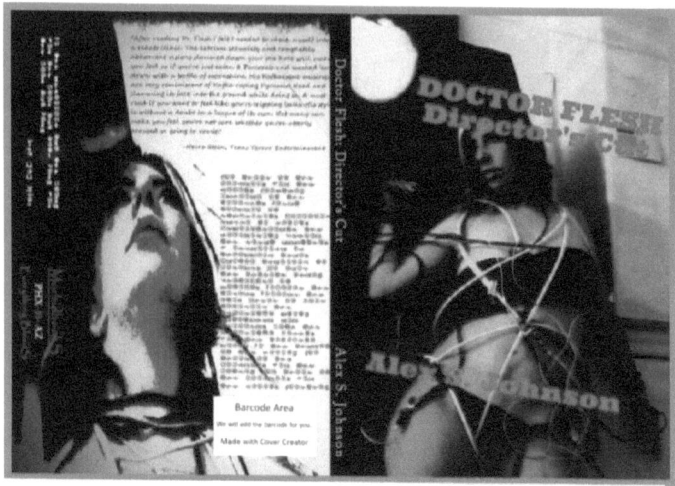

~From Alex S. Johnson, the author of Bad Sunset, Wicked Candy and The Death Jazz, comes a new vision in Bizarro horror. Imagine a TROMA film on meth and acid, one part cyberpunk, one part Franz Kafka, and three parts frankly unsuitable for a sane audience. "Will make you feel as if you've just eaten 8 Percocets and washed 'em down with a bottle of moonshine," says Necro Stein of Texas Terror Entertainment.

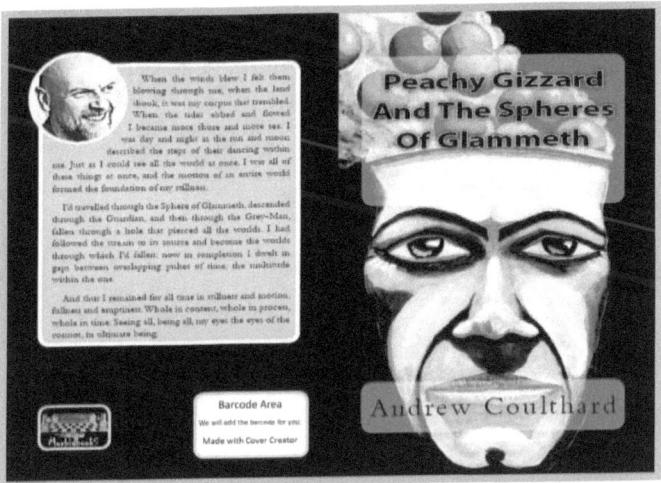

~**When the winds blew i felt them blowing through me,** when the land shook, it was my corpus that trembled. When the tides ebbed and flowed I became more shore and more sea. I was day and night as the sun and moon described the steps of their dancing within me. Just as I could see all the world at once, I was all of these things at once, and the motion of an entire world formed the foundation of my stillness.

I'd travelled through the Sphere of Glammeth, descended through the Guardian, and then through the Grey-Man, fallen through a hole that pierced all the worlds.

~**He had to have her the moment he saw her trachea ring.** Six months later she was his lovely wife. He performed his duties as a husband and she as a wife. He tolerated a house filled with references to her late first husband and the children they had together. He put up with her prudish ways. He waited. He was patient. He planned. He was adaptable. He was rewarded over the course of a week in her basement. He turned his perverse sexual fantasies of worms and maggots and her lovely crusty trachea ring into a gruesome reality.

Welcome To New Edge Hill

~A dirty shameful devil of a secret...

Something that two men share. A legacy that will shock you to
your very core. One that is created not out of madness, but of
the purest desire. Take a vivid journey into the mind of the
killer and his biggest fan. Do you believe in evil? See the knife
plunge. Lap at the wounds. Do you still? There is no rational
meaning or pretty words that will hide away the darkness that
the words of this found journal creates. Inside is the real truth.
And it can set you free. Watch all you want. Taste what you
dare not have.

~"The routine has this inherent tendency to perpetuate lies, and I speak only in thinly veiled euphemisms — hanging out with friends means going to the bar; being tired means too many sleepless nights on amphetamine; going grocery shopping means robbing Price Chopper blind; filling a prescription means visiting my dealer; going to the bank means pawning my possessions — but refer to them not as "lies;" rather, label them as weak excuses utilized to justify my erratic   behaviours.

~**I'm feeling down and dirty, feeling kind of mean,** so I give those fans my middle finger. Those poor bastards go nuts. My team looks at me in awe. My coach frowns and the opposing one begins to furiously scratch out new plays. I see our opponents and I almost feel sorry for the poor bastards. Their fans can't help them. Their coach can't help them. I'm going to run them off their own track in front of their own fans and there is not one thing they can do about it.

~Humanity is the devil is a deconstructed nightmare mixing David Lynch and snuff movies. The plot revolves around a central character, Seth, who is set about a crusade against humanity which, for him, represents pure evil. Through random killings he and his cronies try to accelerate the end of the world, in order to provoke and defeat the Demiurge, the false God that is ruling the earth. As in Burroughs, logical language is replaced here with cut-scenes – sometimes to be taken literally – that plunge the reader into an extreme experience.

Welcome To New Edge Hill

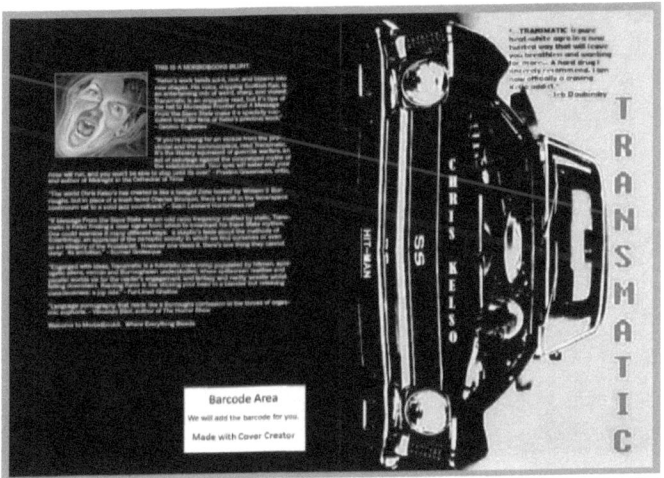

~"As a part-time hitman/ exterminator, Ignius Ellis's dream is to buy a candy-apple red Nova Supreme. In the process of trying to earn enough cash to make his dream come true he gets sucked into the rough world of Visitacion Valley, SF. When the tenants in his apartment complex reveal their various extracurricular activities this take an even more bizarre twist and Ellis soon becomes acquainted with the nightmarish Slave State dimension..."

~That's the last time she gets the bigger worm...

Once their flesh flakes away the angels collapse into puddles of hissing goop and withered petals blow into them hurried along by unseen winds. My spit looses its sweet taste to the black flavor of ash. The glowing birds in the bright orange sky burst into small sparkly novas. The sky itself weeps and tears, streaking down like a ruined painting as the dismal grey of life wheezes back before my eyes. I don't blink; praying silently for one last desperate sensation of the high. Lila feels it too. She writhes on the mattress next to me...

~Within these twisted and perverted pages, Johnson manages to demolish clichés with a jaded finesse that I've personally never encountered in written form. Another apparent talent is his effortless deconstruction of pop-culture allegories and references as found in his story "Vampussy." No one is safe or spared from his dagger sharp sarcasm and wit.
While not without its flaws, my appreciation for this kind of talent and voice is what made his writing so fun to read, even if he might possibly be out of his ever-loving mind.

~**In Garrett Cook's Murderland serial killers are idolized by society.** Their deeds are followed obsessively by television pundits and the adoring public. A subculture has grown up around this phenomena, called "Reap." Laws are created to allow this activity to flourish, including designated "safe zones' where killers can practice their trade without fear of persecution. Fans of the top rated serial killers celebrate each new kill on social media and television. Programs glorify their deeds.

The culture of Murderland is violent and mirrors our own violent society and its decadent obsessions.

~Born whole from the rectum of a dying patient, Morbid silently stalks the hospital's hallways, heinously dispatching the most helpless of patients and in the most painfully repulsive of manners. In the meantime, in order to pay for his family and home that includes his ghost step-father Sammy and his pet aborted fetus Chip, Westphal has to ingest mounds of dangerous narcotics to get through his night shifts. Barely hanging on to his Care Tech gig by his fingernails, the last thing Westphal needs is to be accused of Morbid's evil deeds. You, on the other hand, simply seek some solace from all Your diseases

Dani Brown

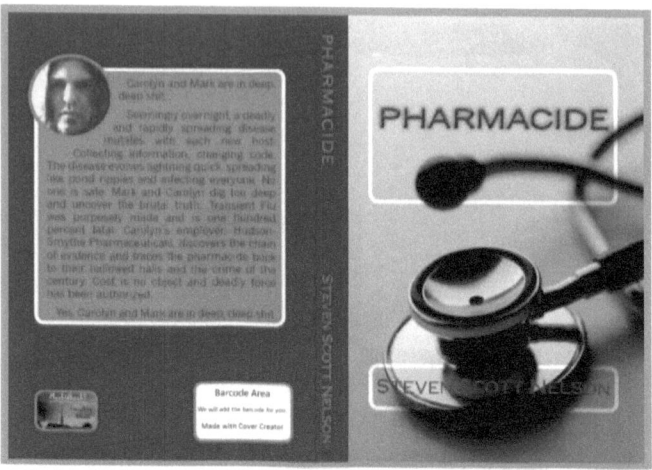

~**It looks like Carolyn and Mark are in deep, deep shit...** Mark
and Carolyn live in an alternate 1989 where Ronald Reagan is
on his fourth presidential term. The USA has a rigid, long-
standing caste system and abortions were never made legal.
Being homeless is a crime that is punishable by imprisonment
in Tent City. Most of Mark's ER patients are inmates at this
camp and are victims of a new disease dubbed Transient Flu.
This deadly and rapidly spreading disease mutates with each
new host, collecting information, changing code. The disease
evolves lightning quick, spreading like pond ripples...

~IMMANUEL THE CHRIST has some nerve. Jonah has already lost everyone he loves to Pilate the vampire and his Harbor drug violence. Jonah now trudges through his days staying as high on Plata as possible. He just wants to be left alone while he waits for his turn to die. The Christ has other plans for him. She sends Pedro, to assign Jonah to order the Herod to dismantle the Harbor's Plata trade. Jonah decides to run. But you can't run from God. As Jonah learns the hard way when the 'Edmund Fitzgerald' goes down in rough seas, with the reluctant prophet on board...

Dani Brown

~**Five Very Wicked Shorts.** Brought to you with love and blood from The Grim Reverend Steven Rage, the 'Most Depraved Writer in Print'. ~

Through the sheer shock of his presentation, Rage forces readers to consider the alternatives, to look at the garbage in the streets, to see what is swept into the gutters at night right before all decent people awake to see another cleaned up version of the day. Depravity at its finest, but really the stories are loads of fun.

~Pontius Pilate is cursed to be a vampire. Life after life after life.~ And for the Plata dealing Pilate, his life is more like a death sentence. His only chance surviving is to keep on selling his monthly quota of Plata. This new man-made narcotic is a potent speed-ball designed to amp up the user, while also numbing the conscience into euphoric oblivion. To nullify the pain. To stifle the torture. To run and to hid from all the anguish inside. PILATE is a drug lord vampire in this re-telling of Christ's final days.

~**Following religious folklore, parables, and beliefs,** Rage presents the readers with a God who truly is the Shepherd that leaves no sheep behind. While this tale is deeply woven with the intricacies of a dark, drug-infested world ruled by evil forces, this is the story of a lost sheep. All are God's children, even the most foulest of evil creatures who by their own will have become so through their spiritual and physical copulation with the Devil, and as such, in God's mercy, still are given a chance to be saved.

~During the height of England's Bubonic Plague an ancient Evil Force strolls into London-Town in the form of a would-be doctor. It could smell the blood from miles away, wanting only to help. At the hospital where he cares for the victims of this Black Death, the ill come to him unimpeded. They arrived and fell by the scores. With the help of his ever-faithful assistant, Sightless Agnes, a most ravenous cares for them all. Eating his way through an entire hospital, he treats them until there is nothing left. Nothing save their empty eye sockets, a few pounds of leeched bleached bones and some bolts of old dried-out flesh-leather parchment.

Dani Brown

~New from MorbidbookS: Where Everything Bleeds is an instant collector's specimen and a certain stunner. ~ Be the first freak on your block to acquire this singular and unexpurgated exquisite culling of The Grim Reverend Steven Rage's favourite 'meds'. Enjoy this one-of-a-kind vivid look into the twisted mind of The Most Depraved Writer In Print as he captains you through the intoxicating stain of his wicked imagination. Included are numerous Photos, Paintings and Illustrations embellished with dramatic grayscale that enhance these iniquitous and magnificent Dark Fantasy fables.

Welcome To New Edge Hill

~Click On Image For More DANI BROWN On Kindle~